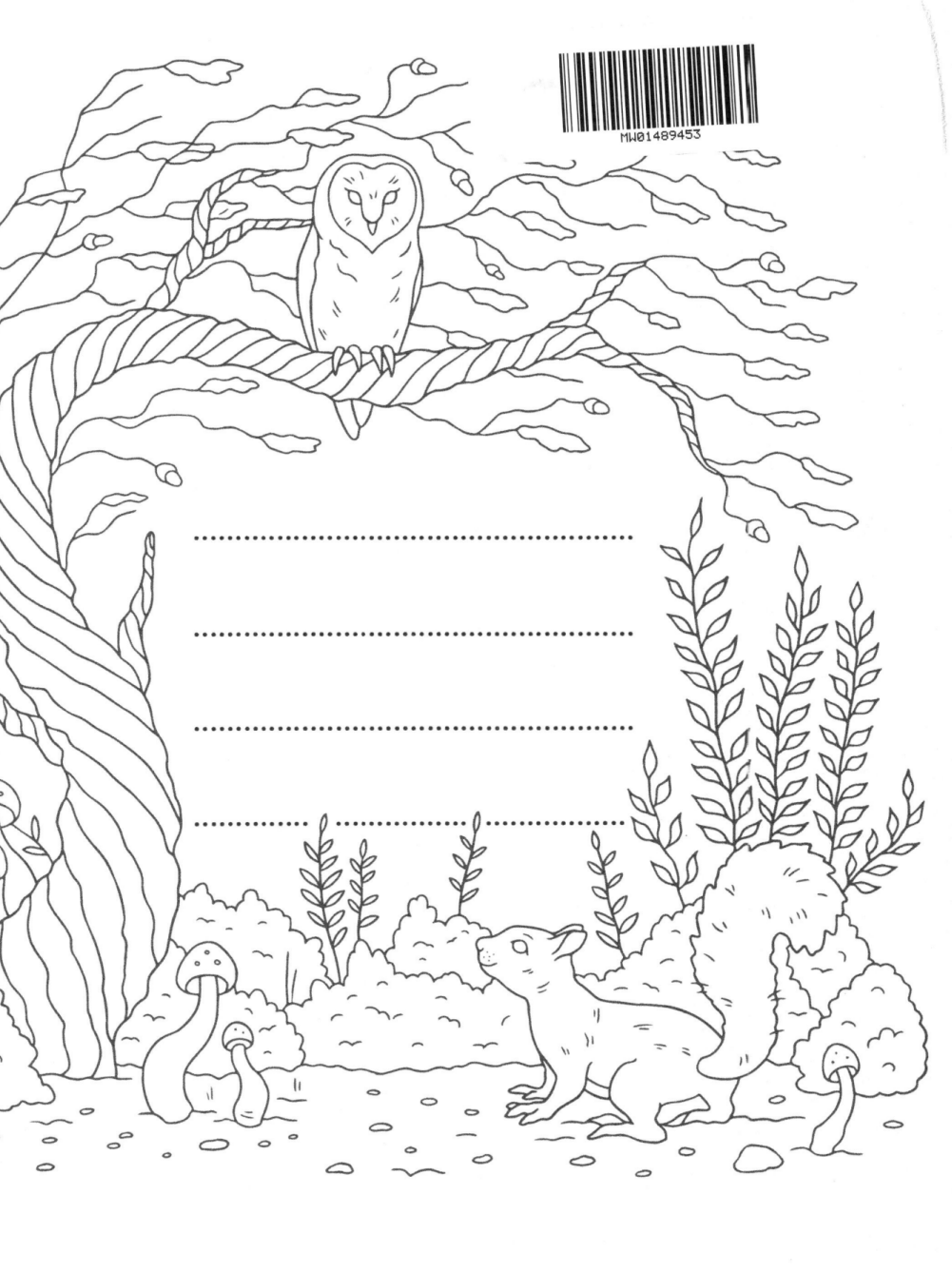

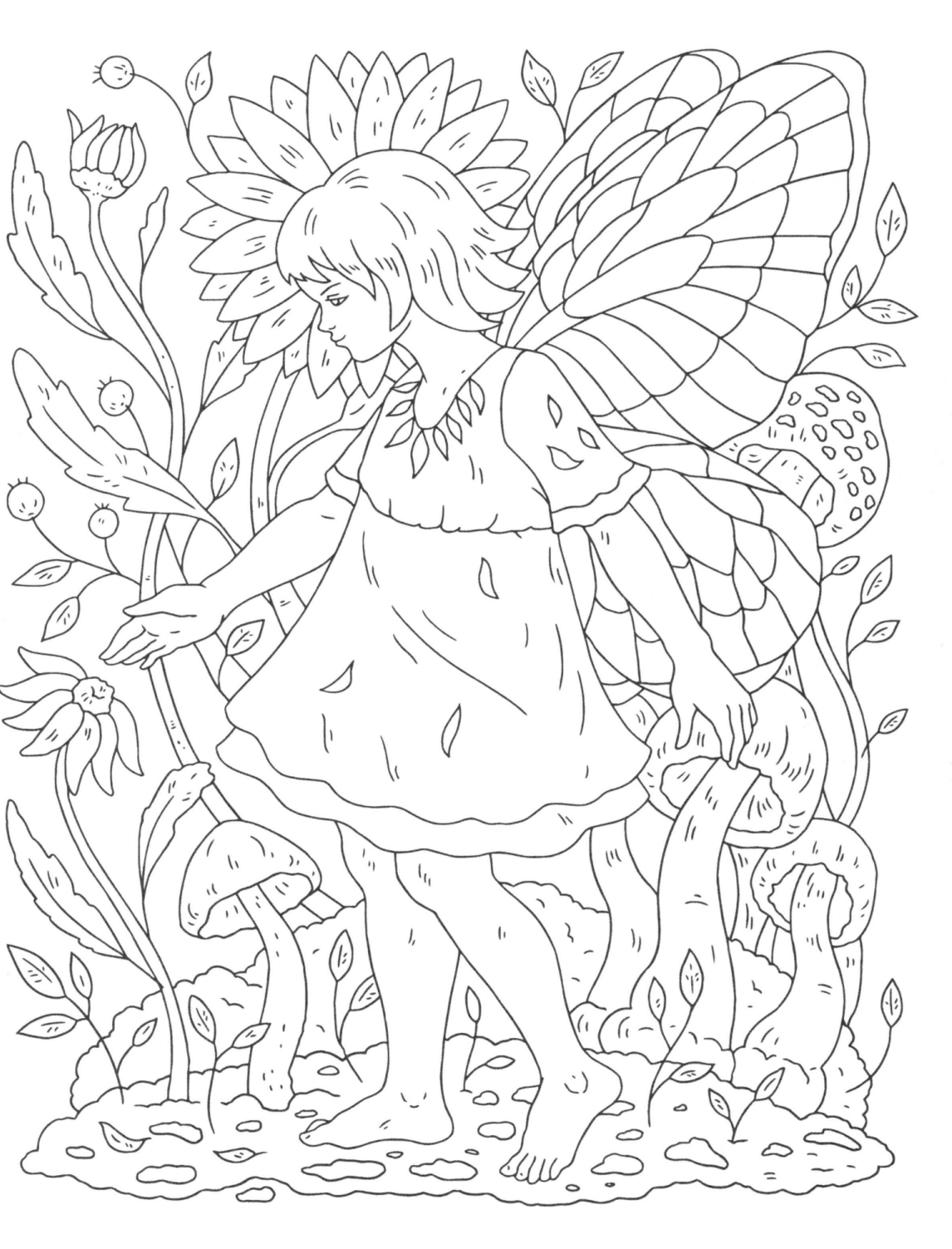

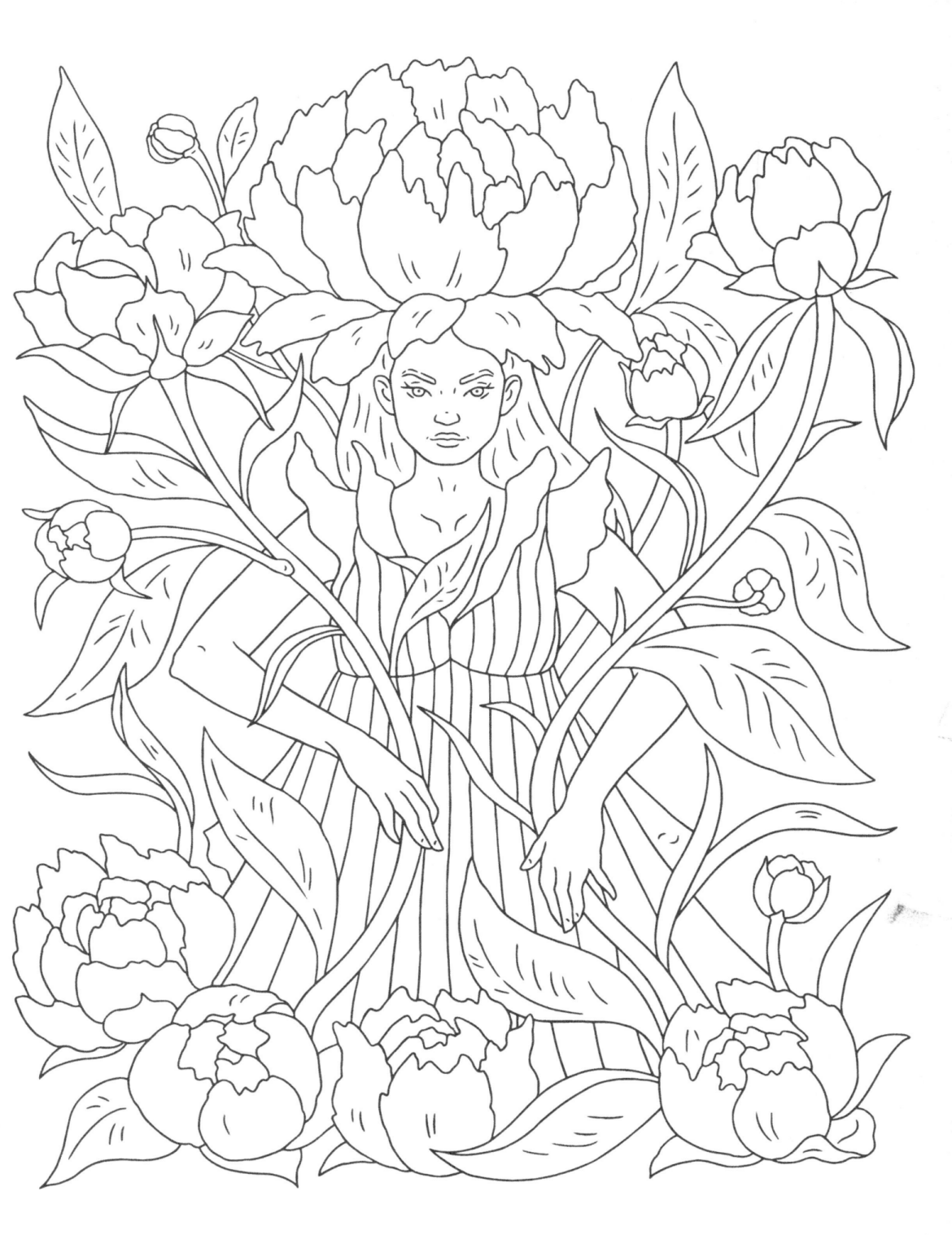

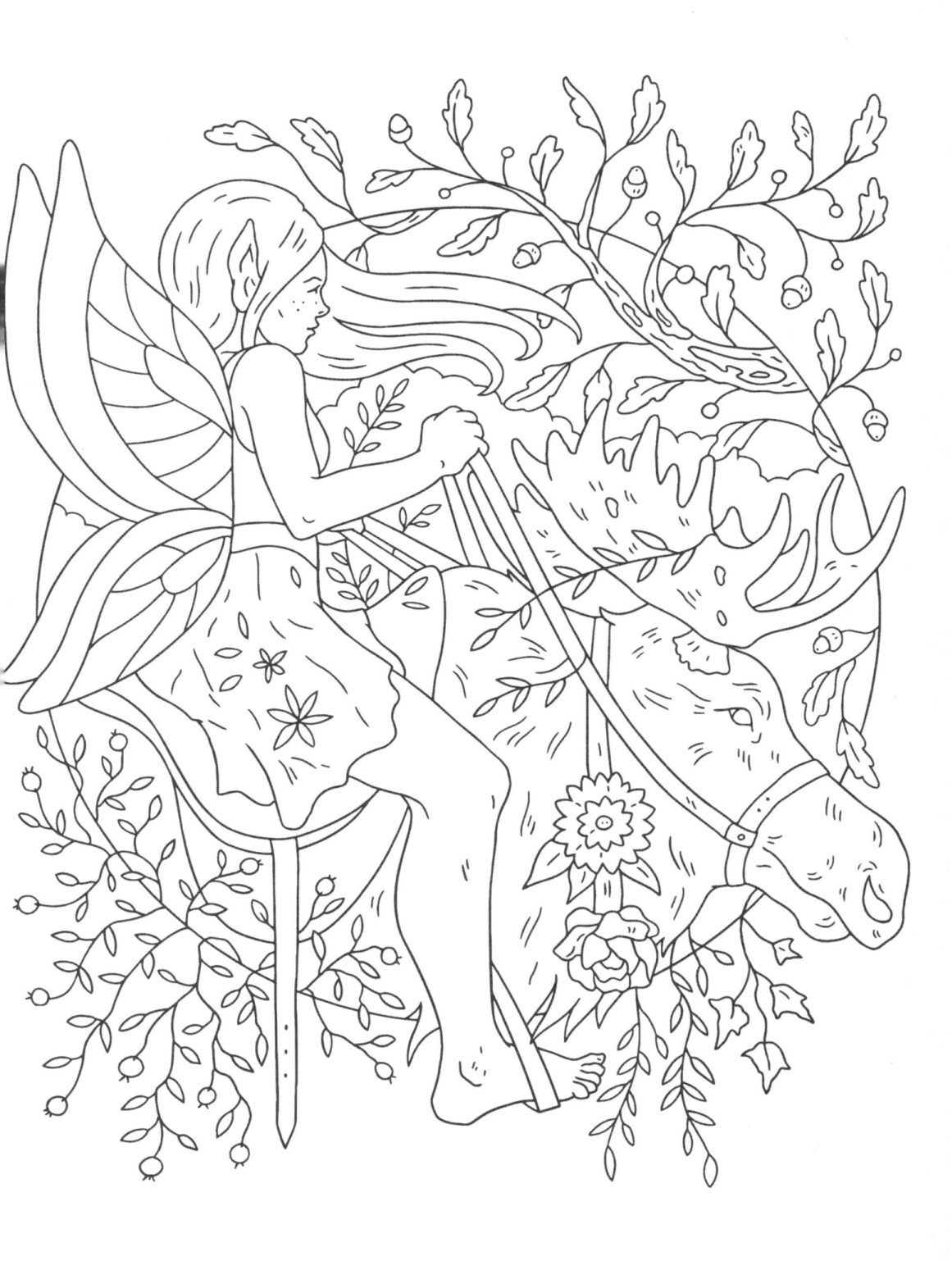

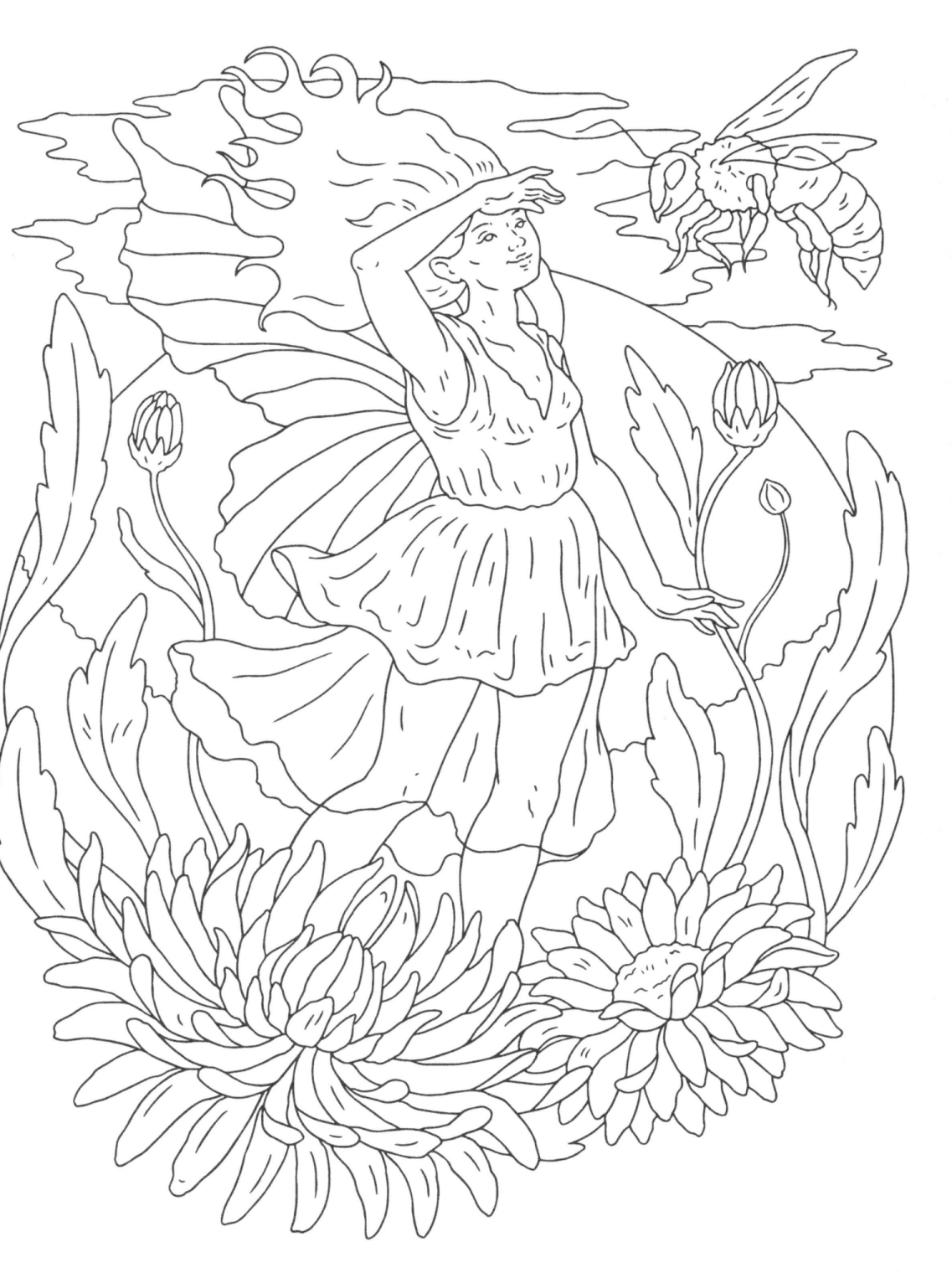

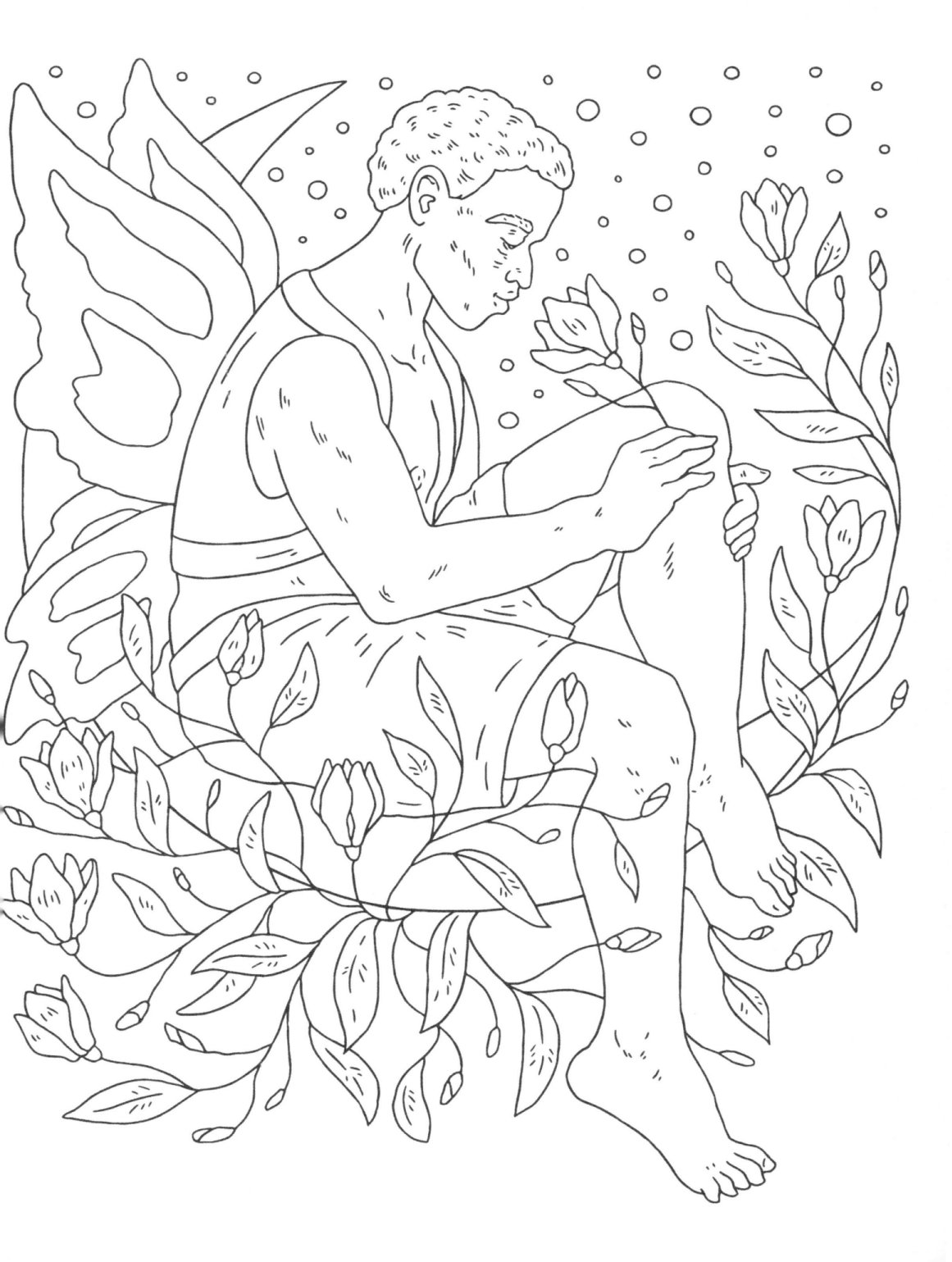

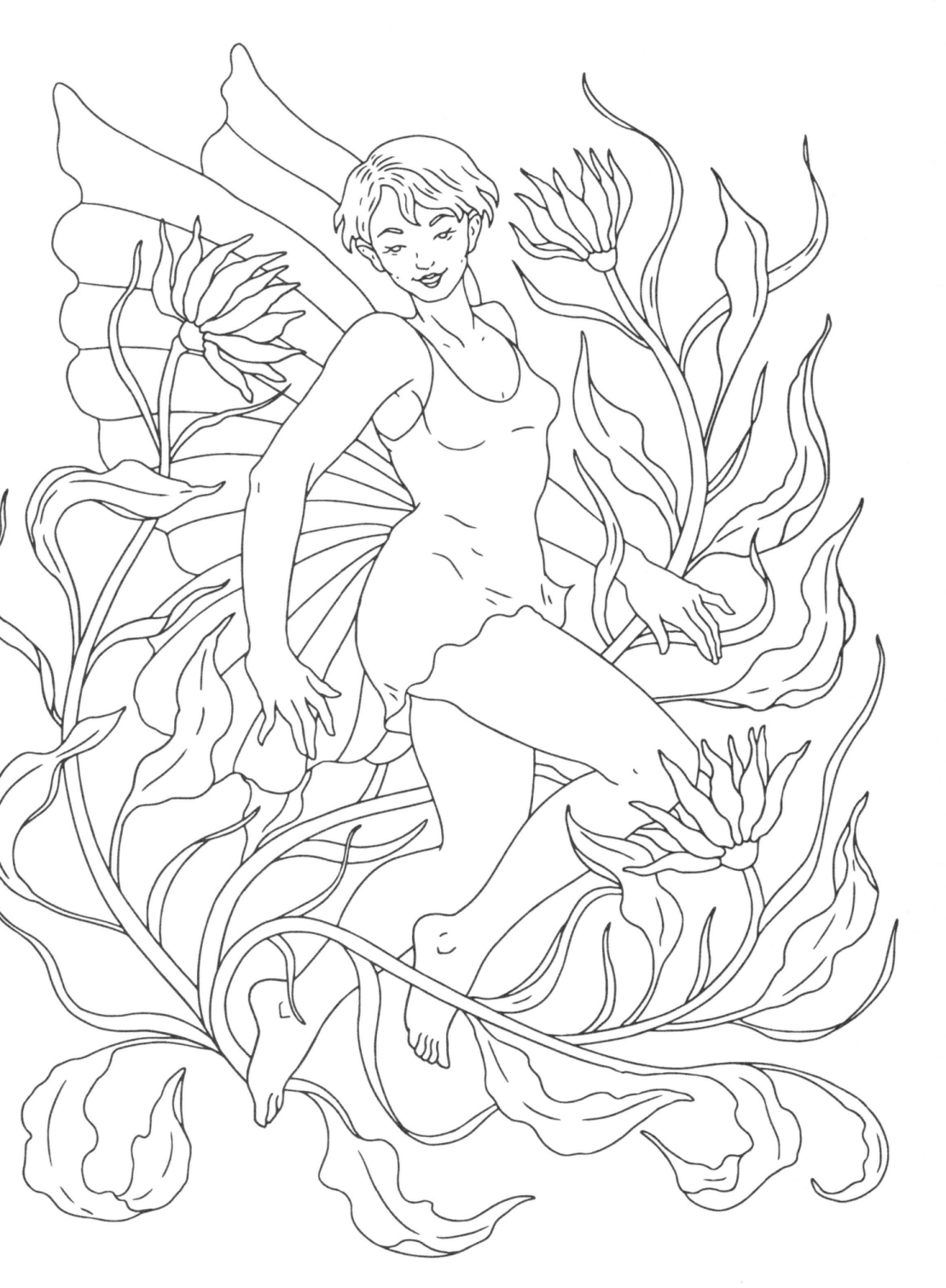

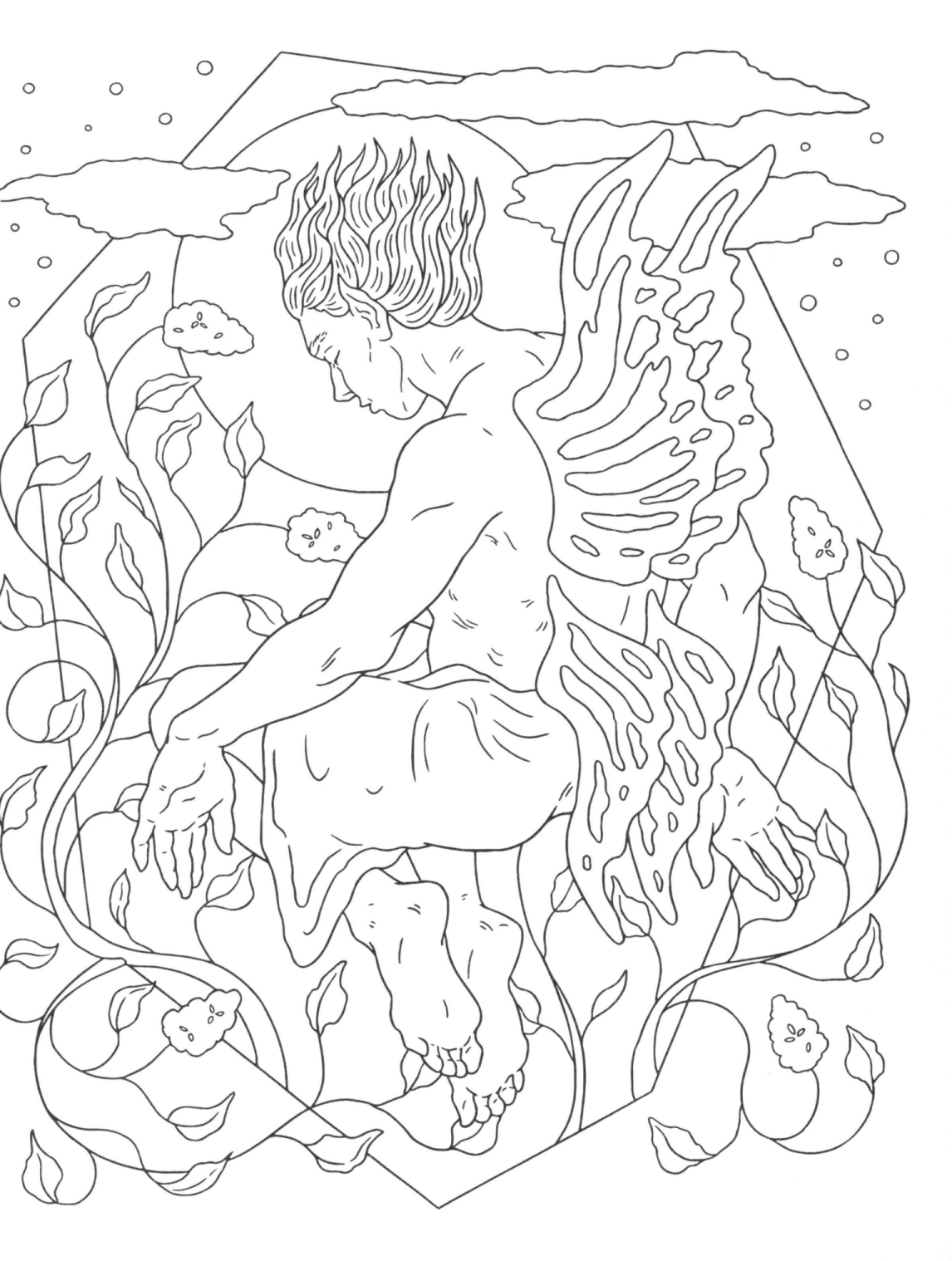

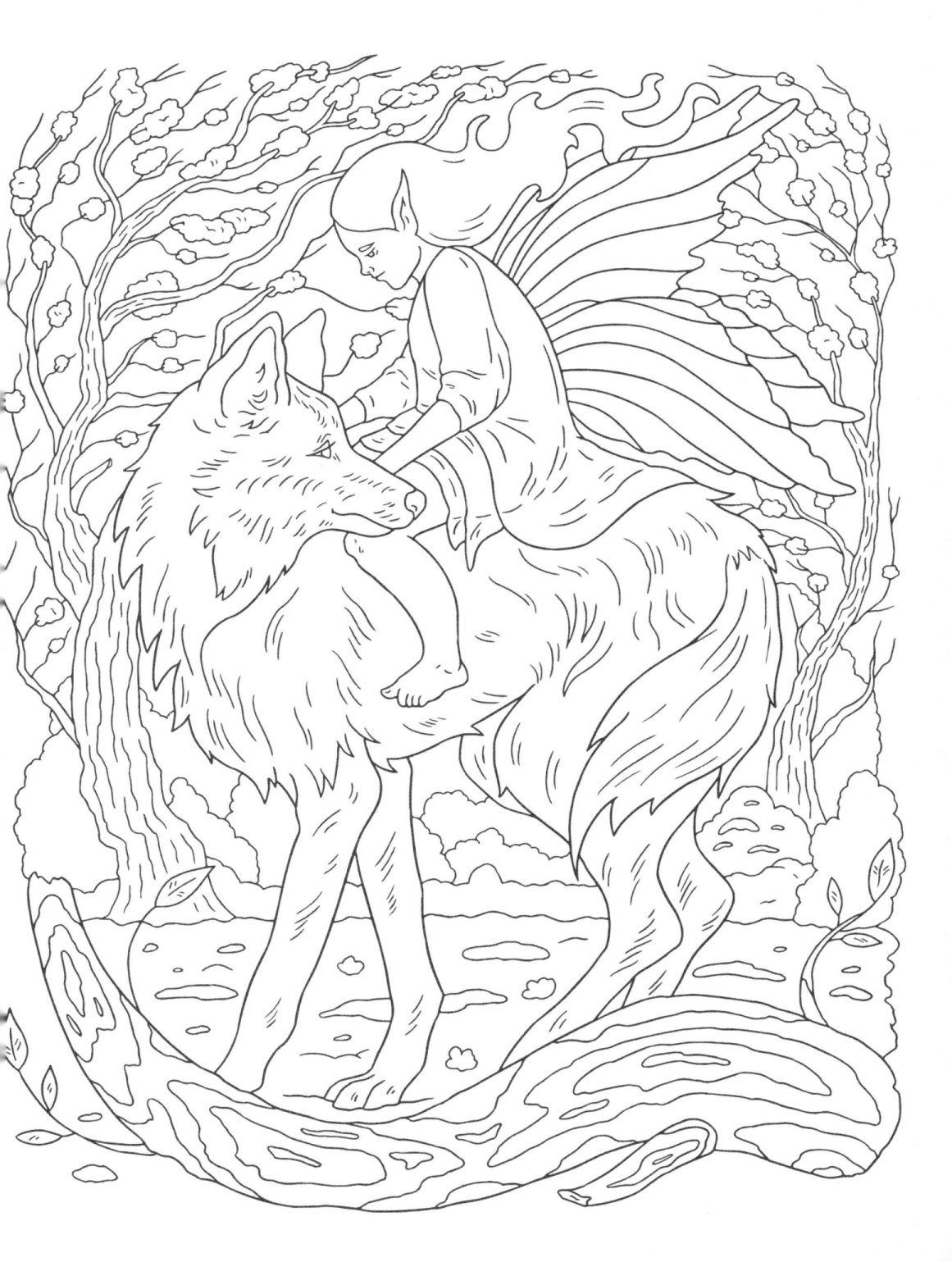

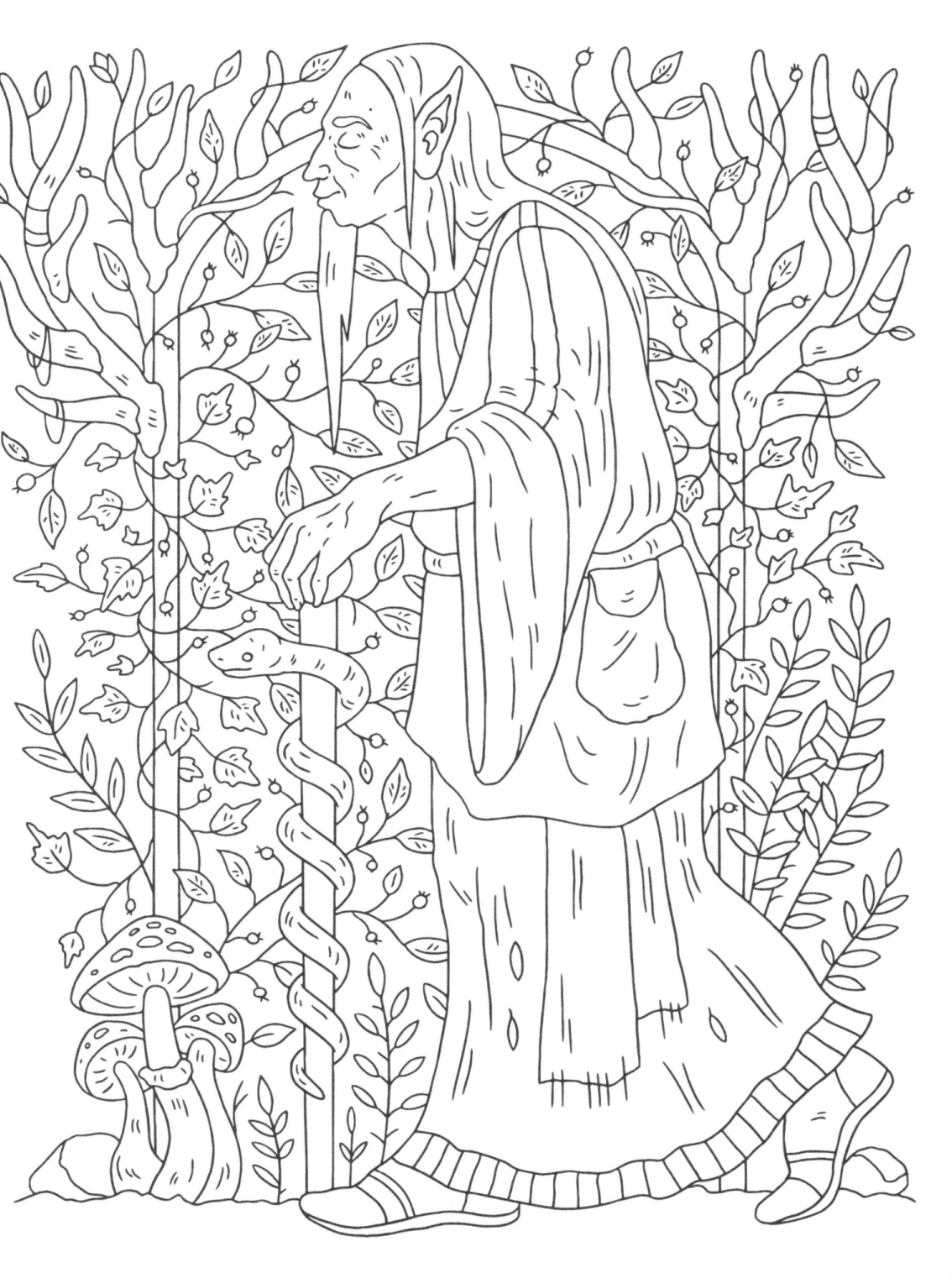

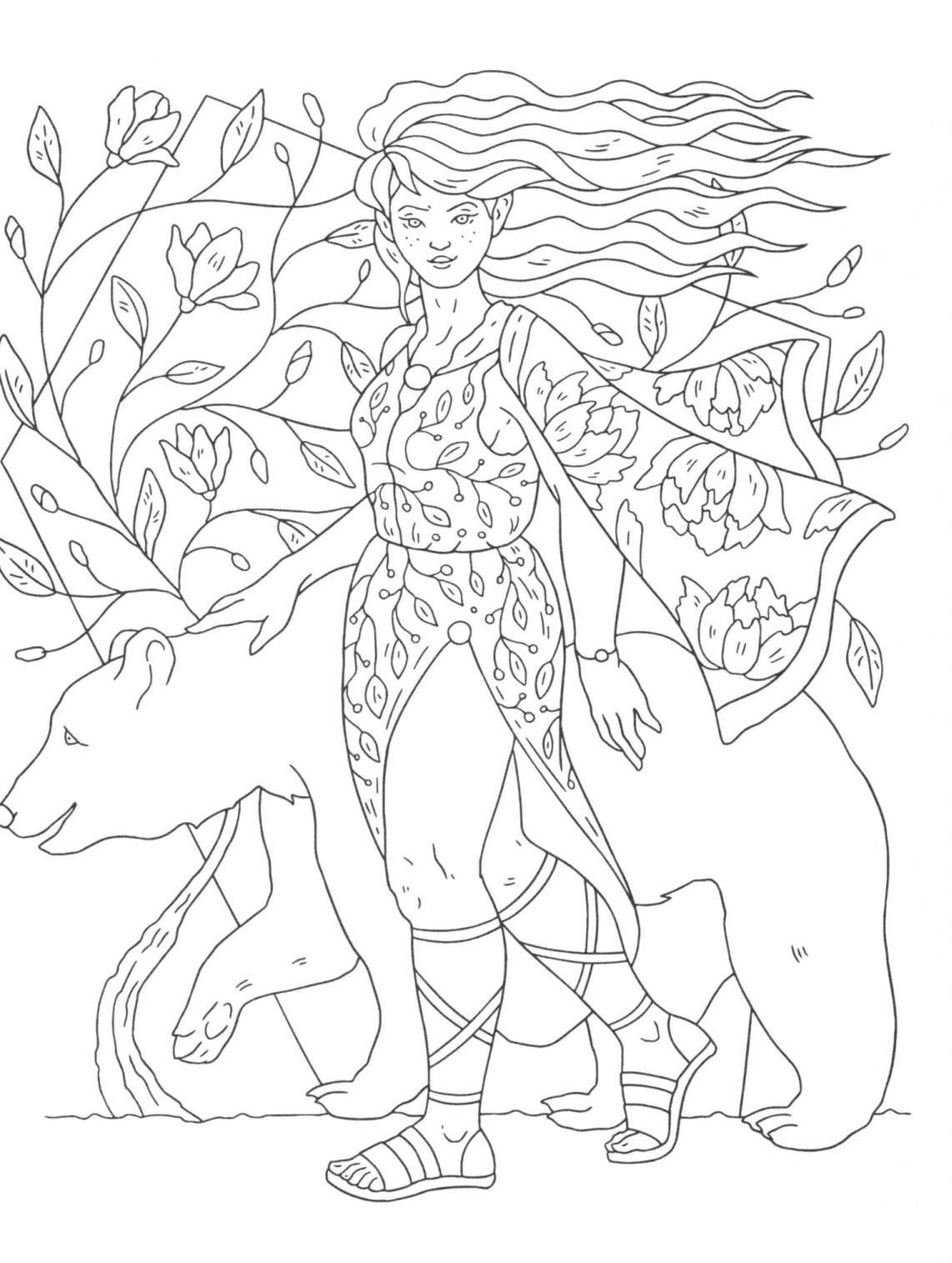

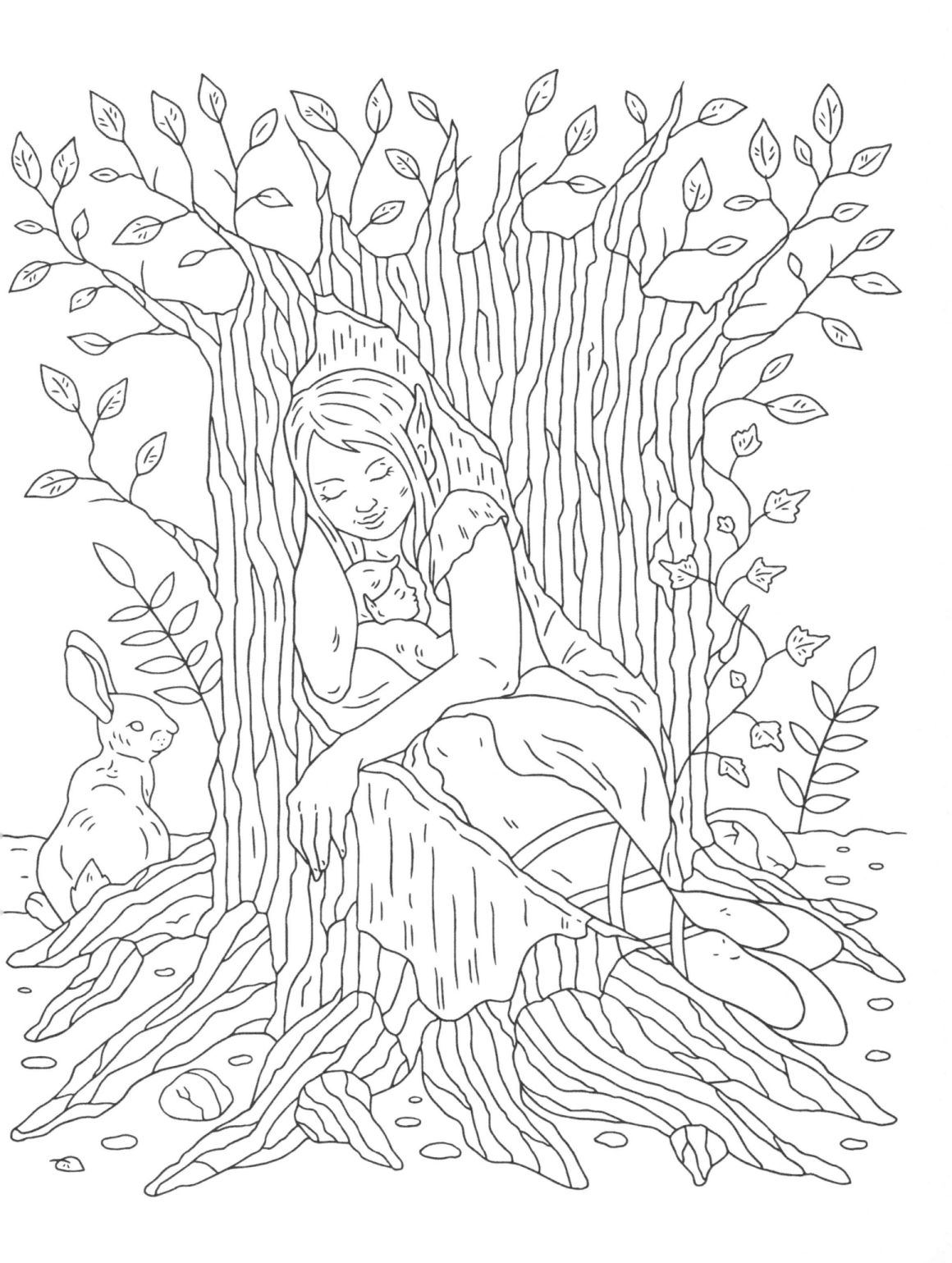

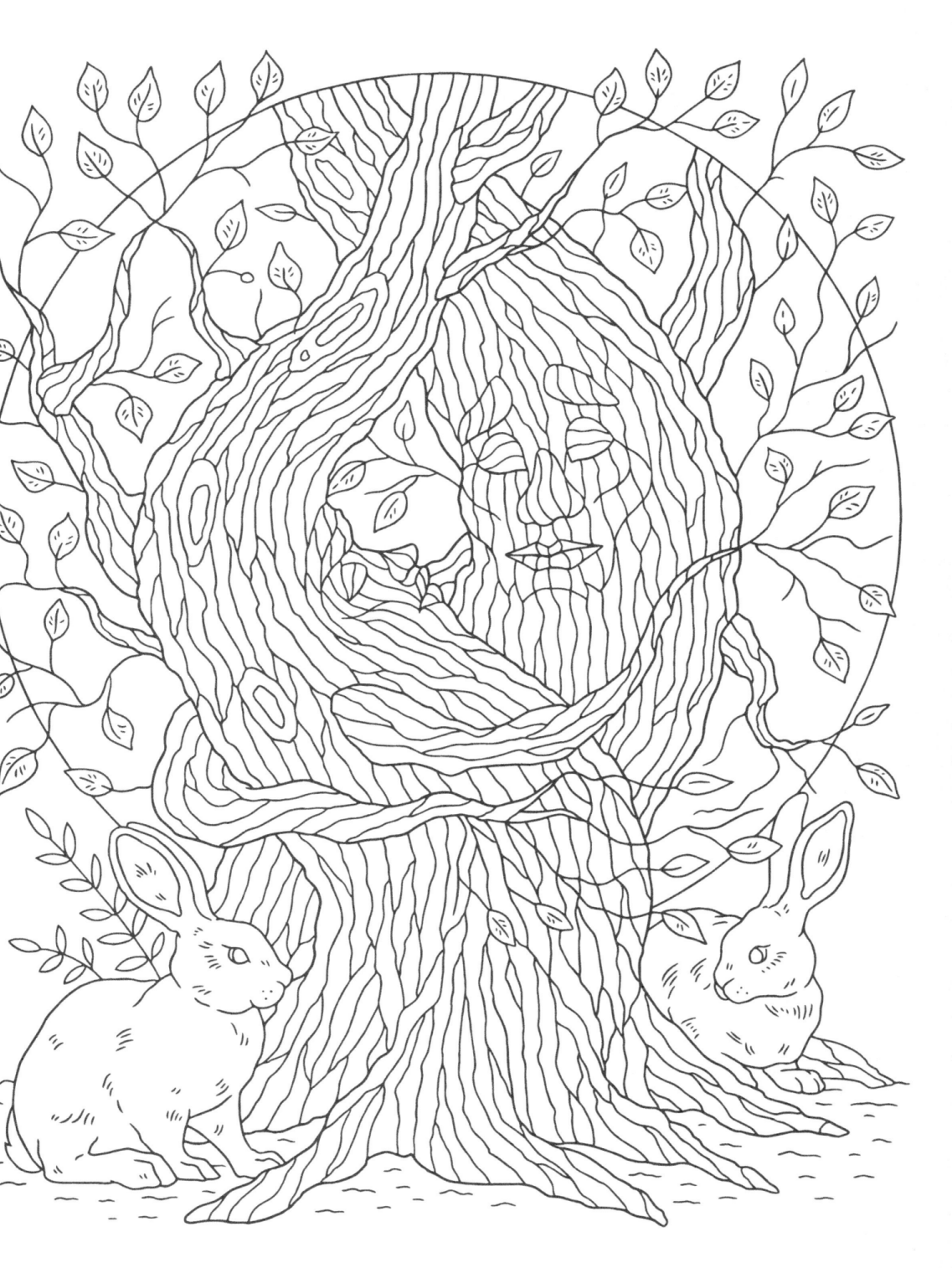

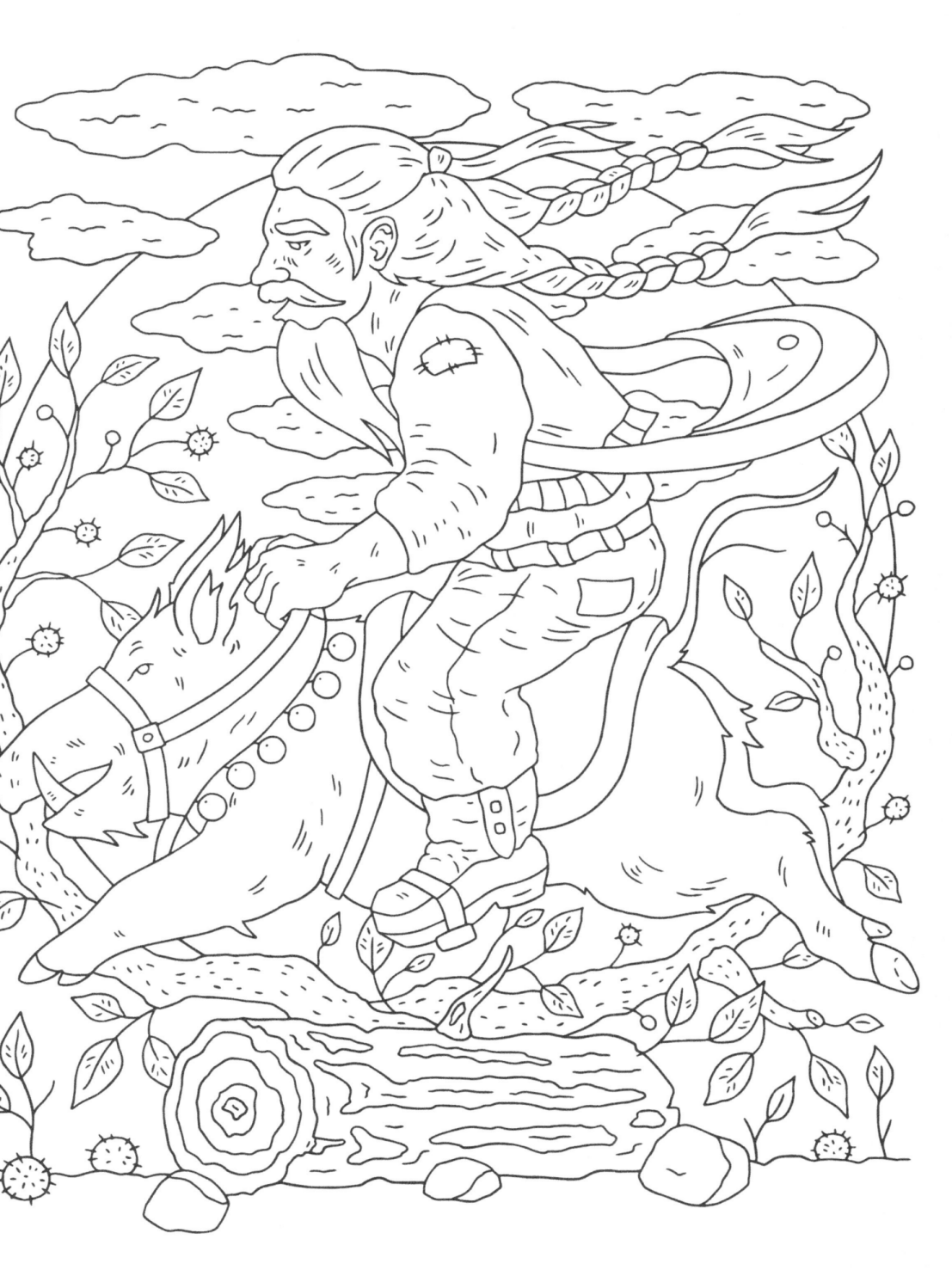

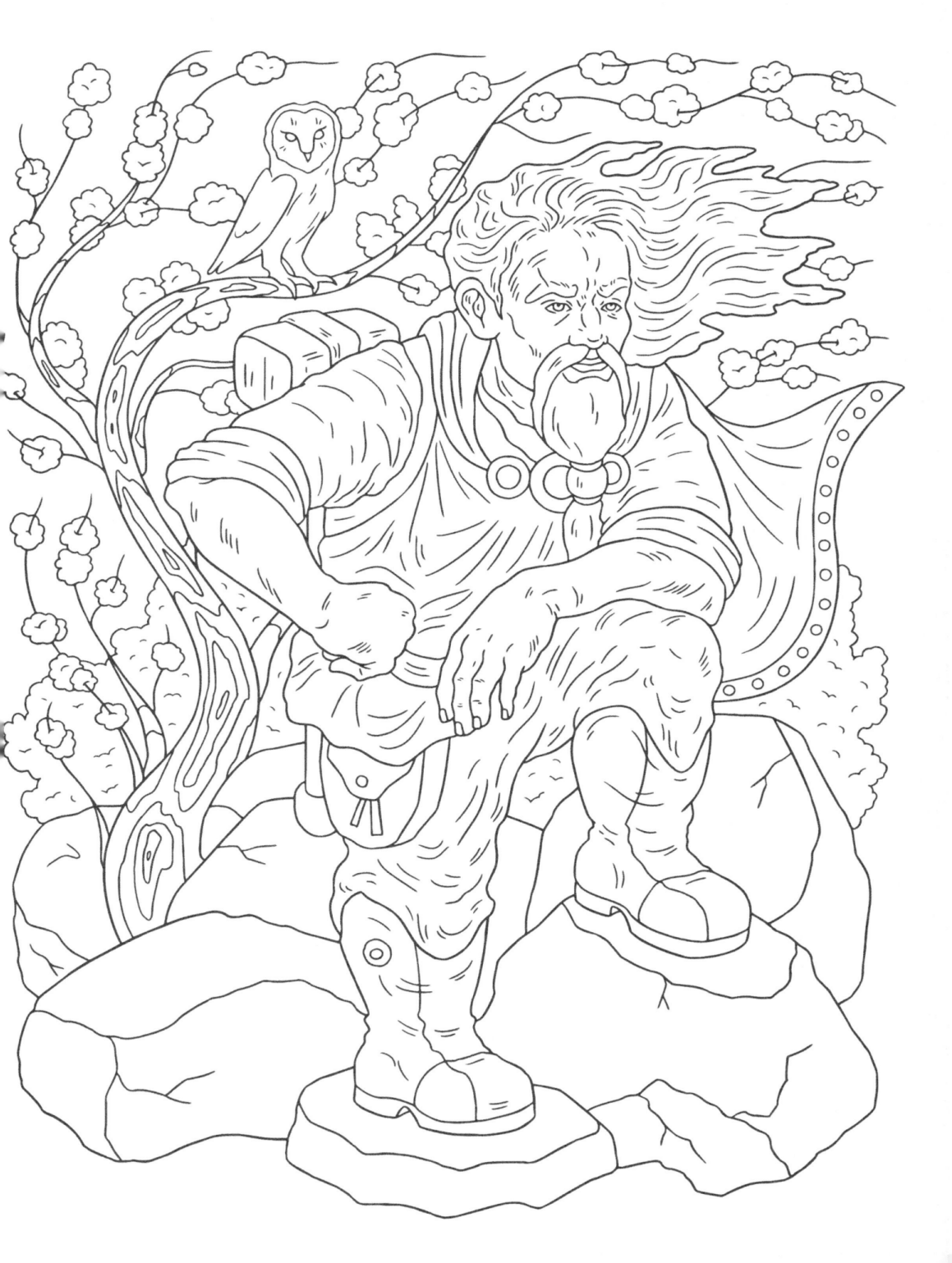

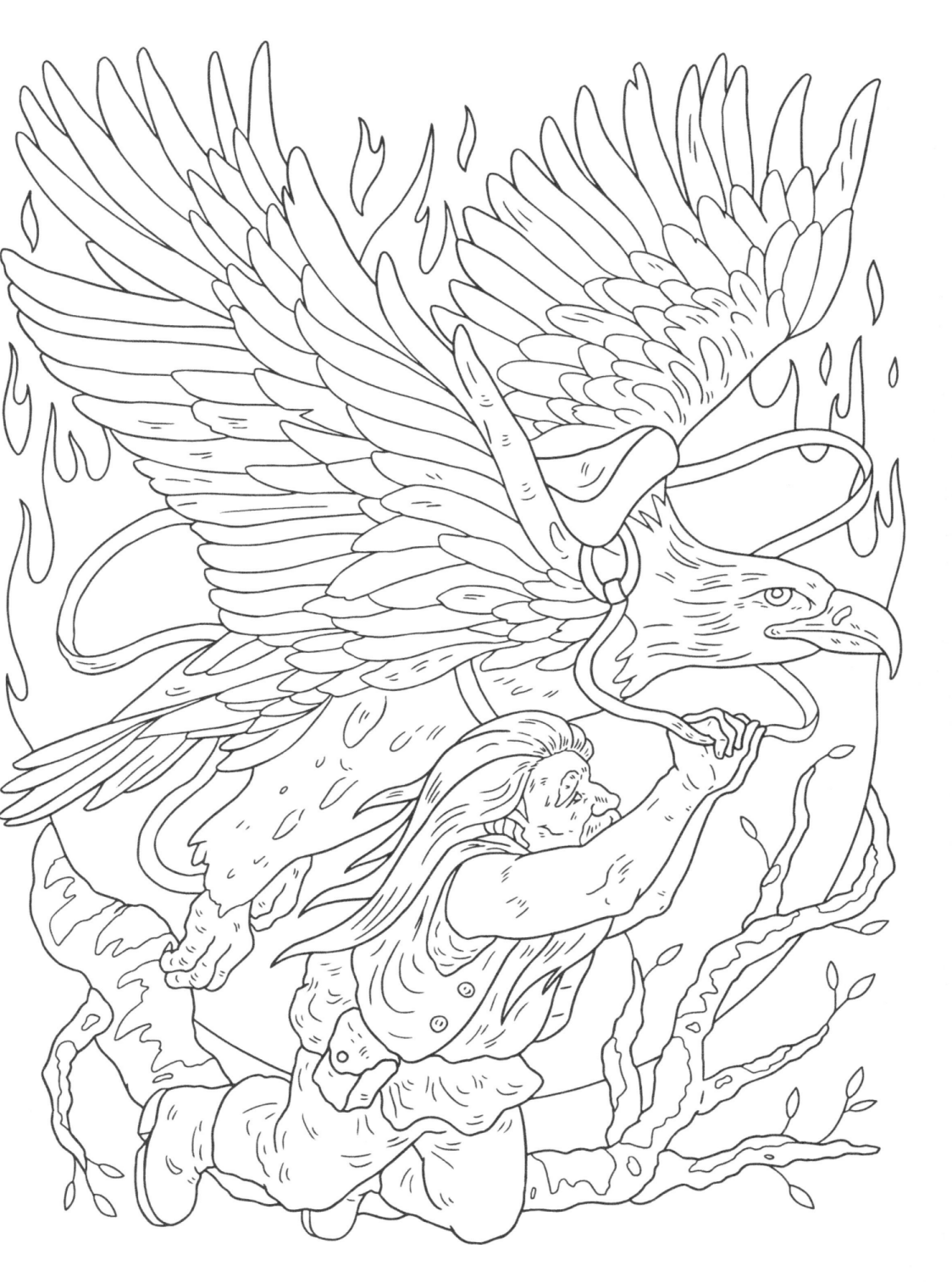

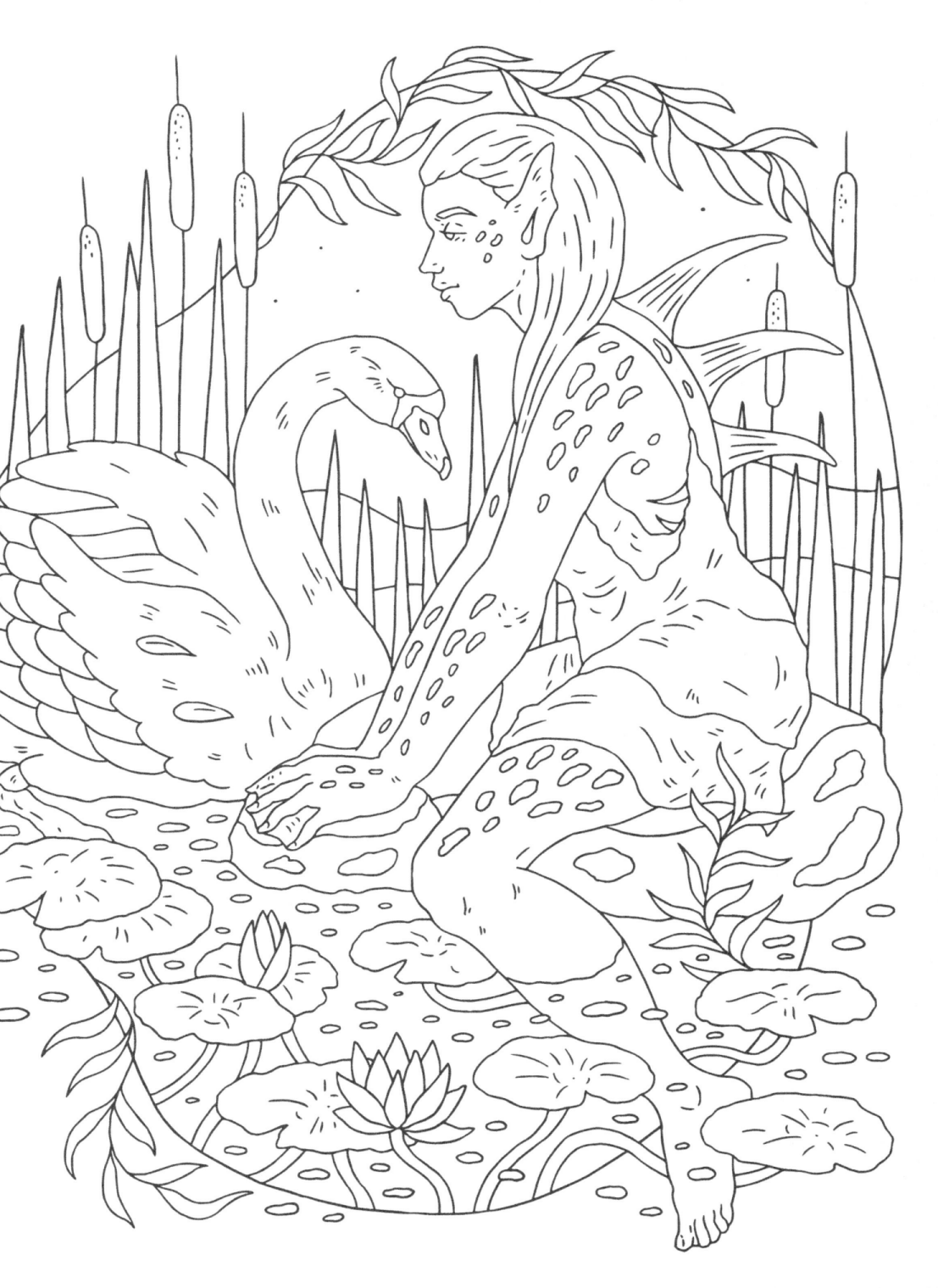

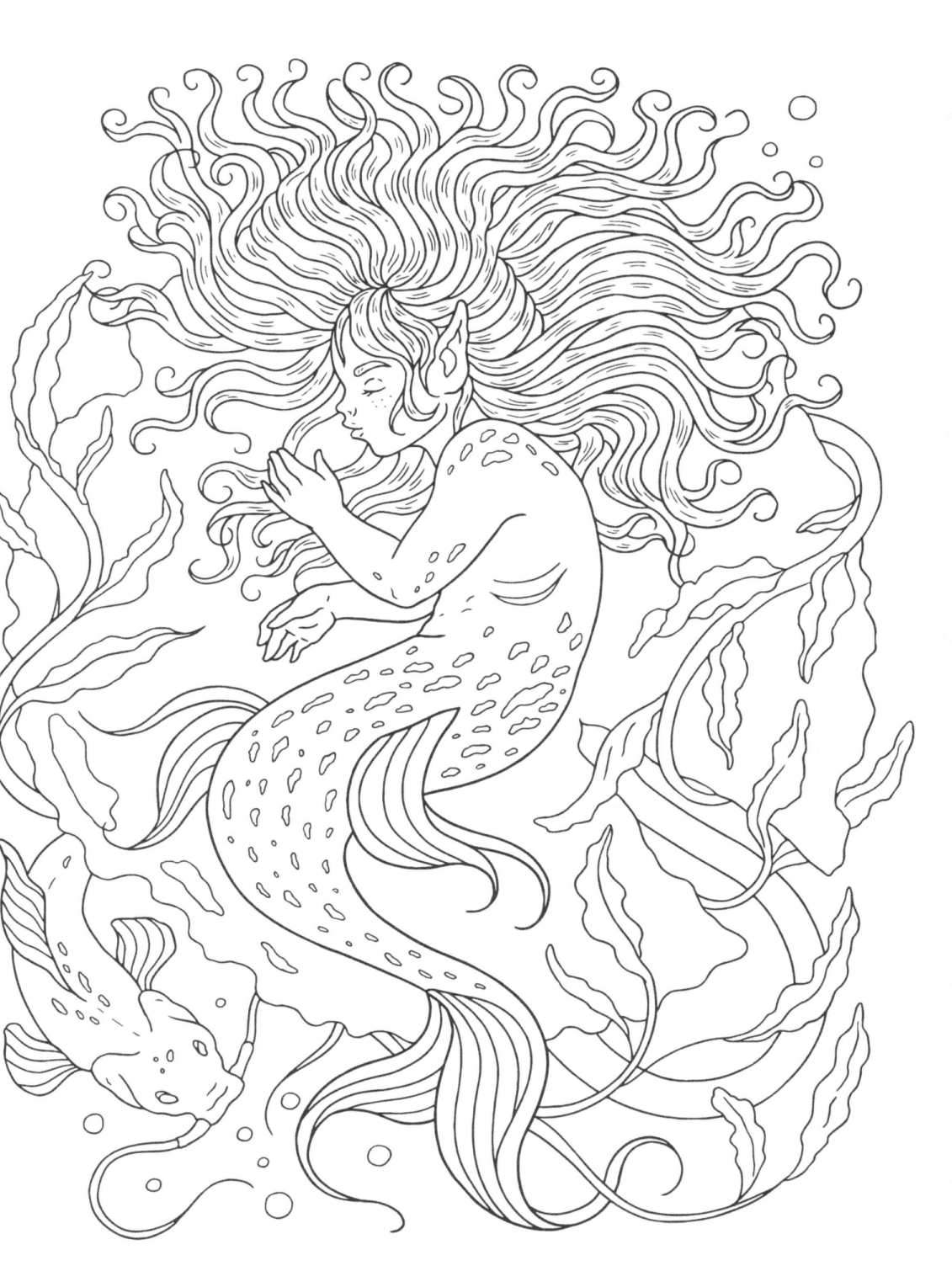

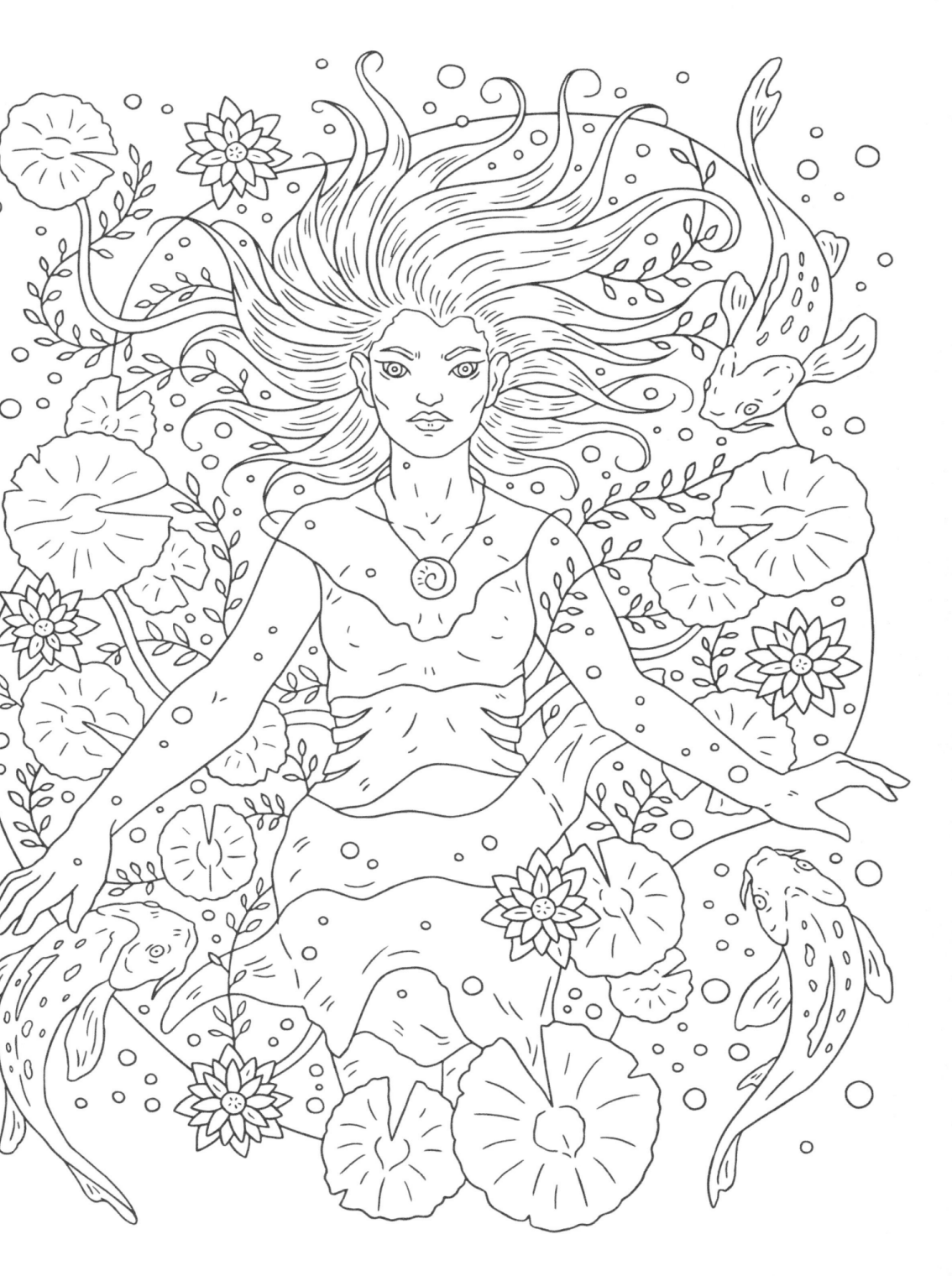

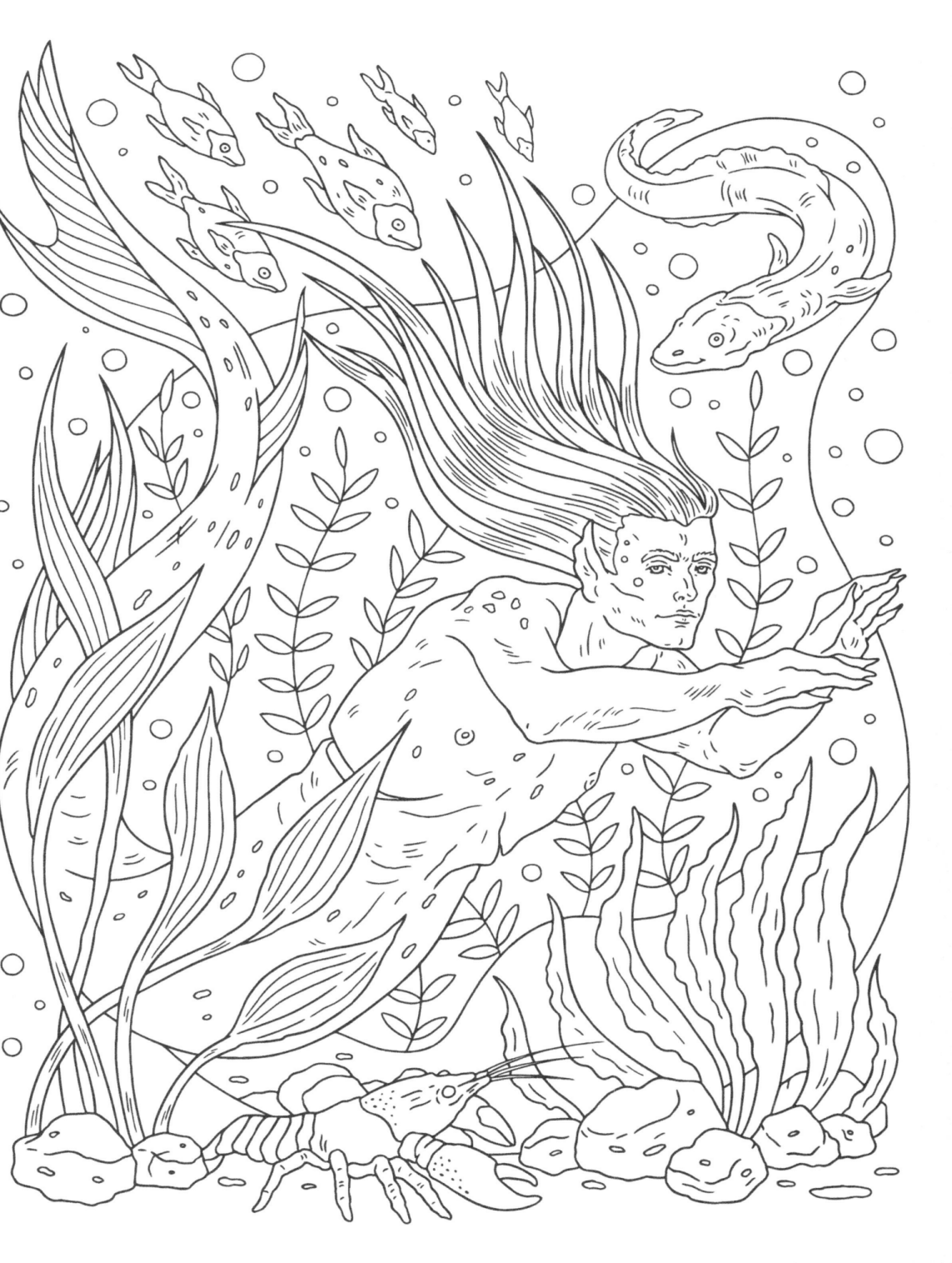

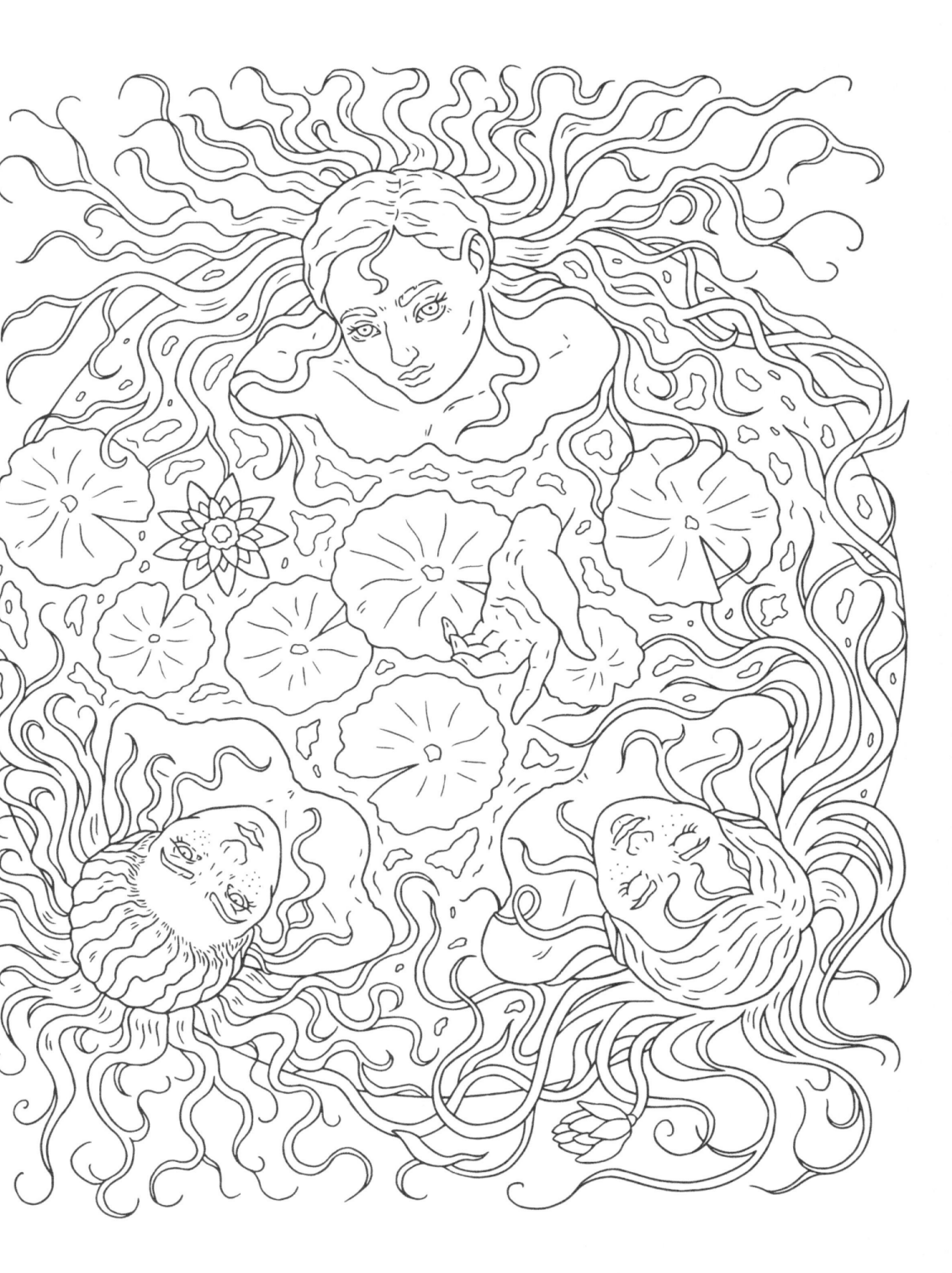

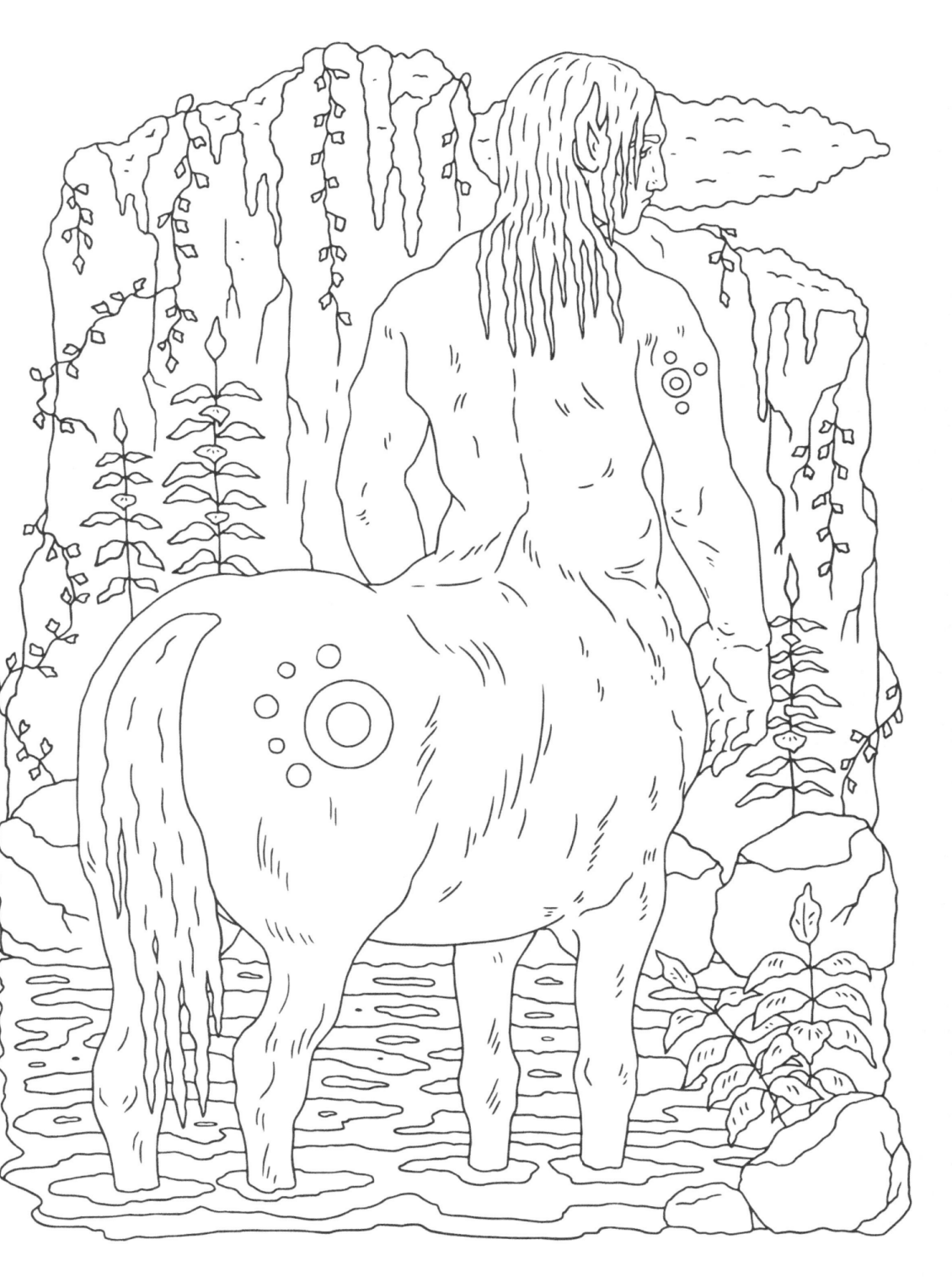

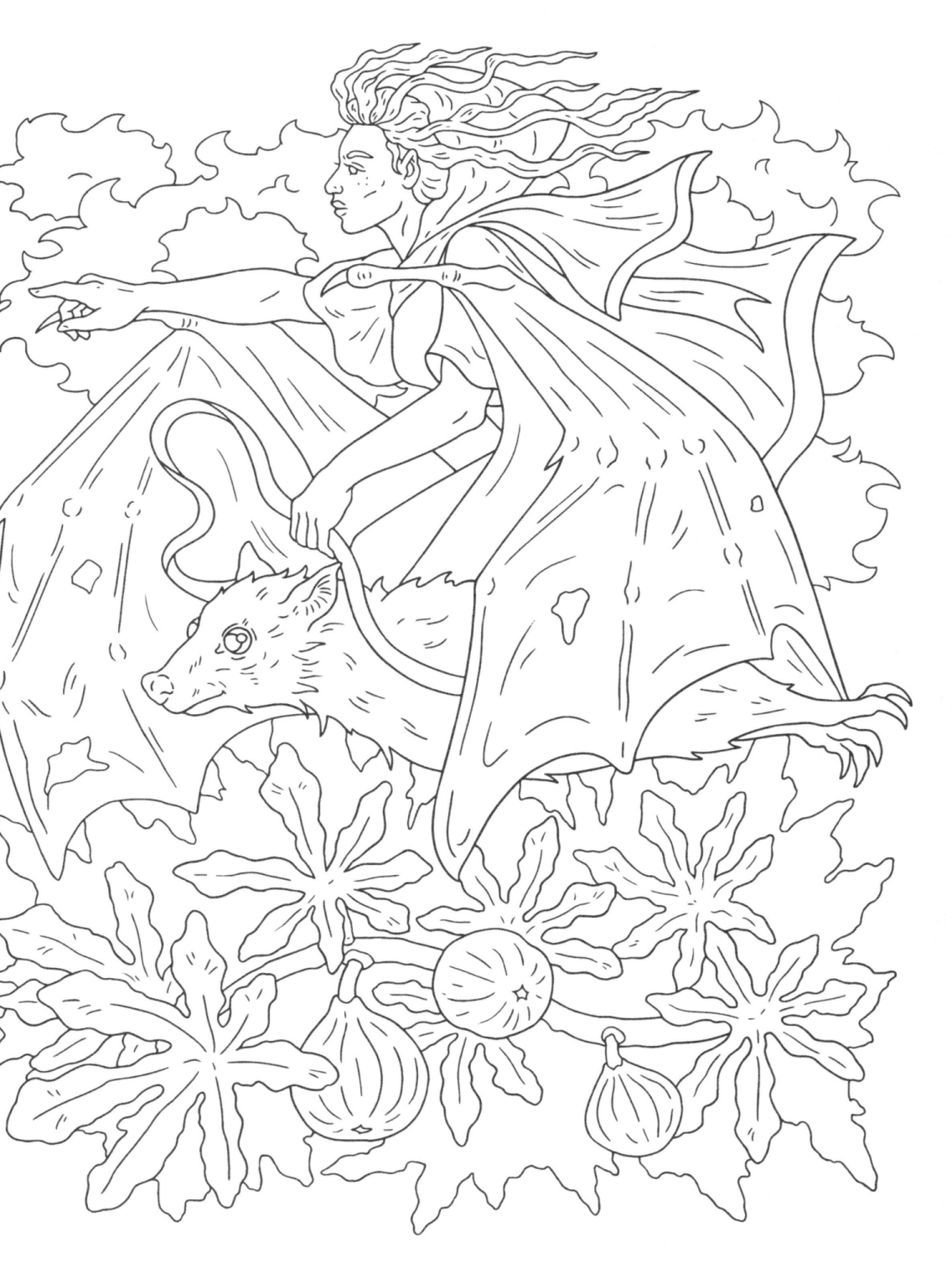

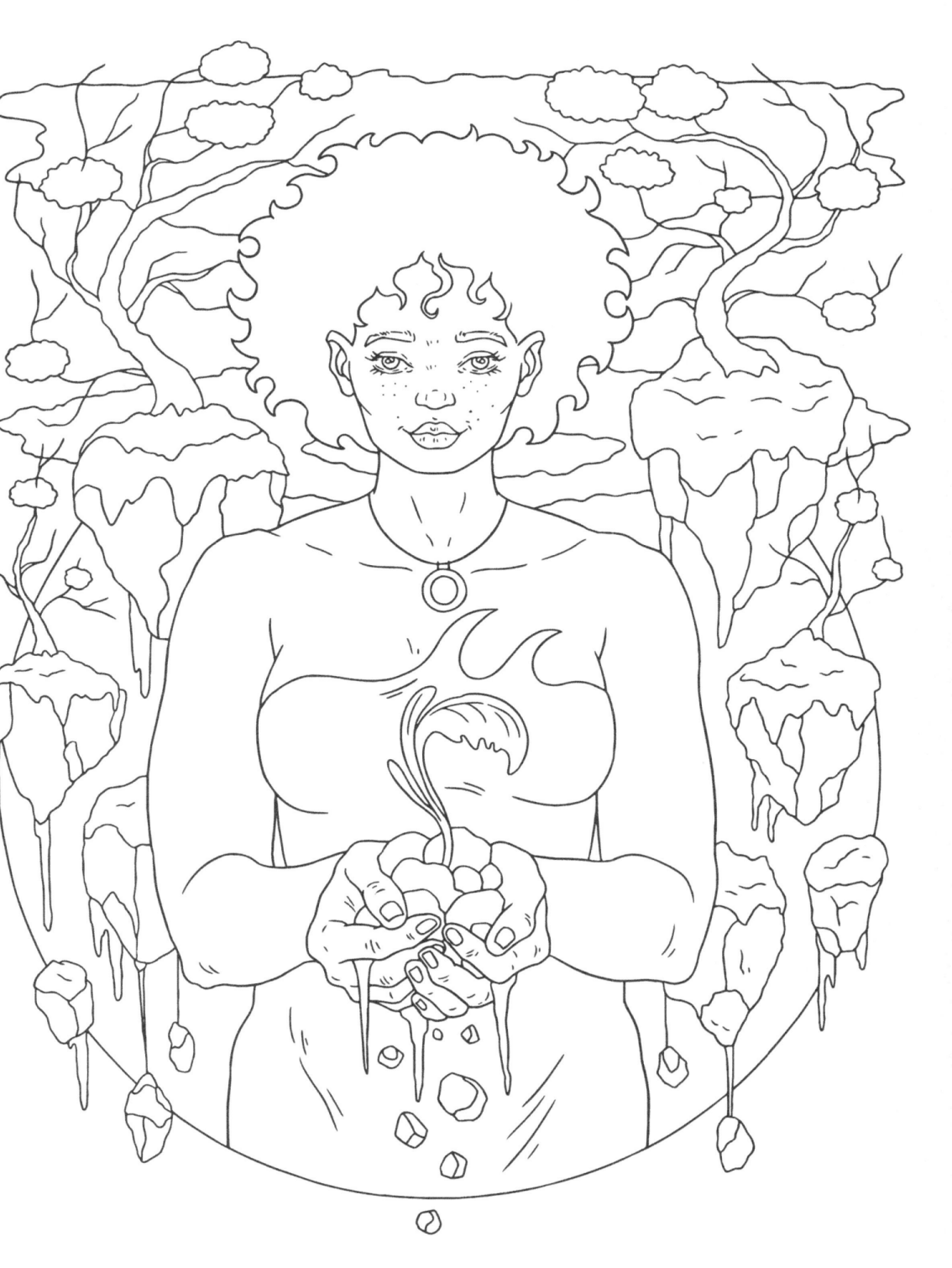

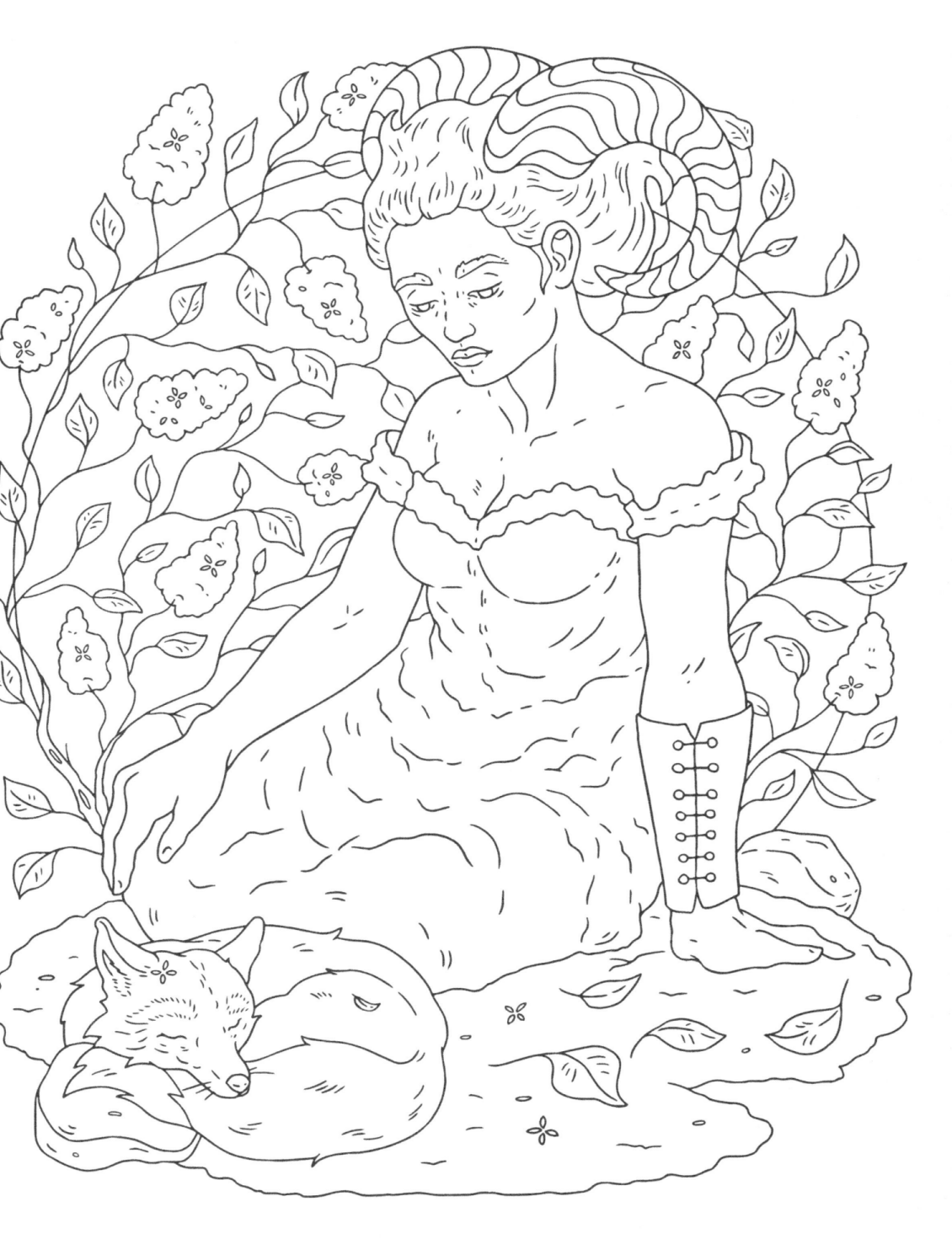

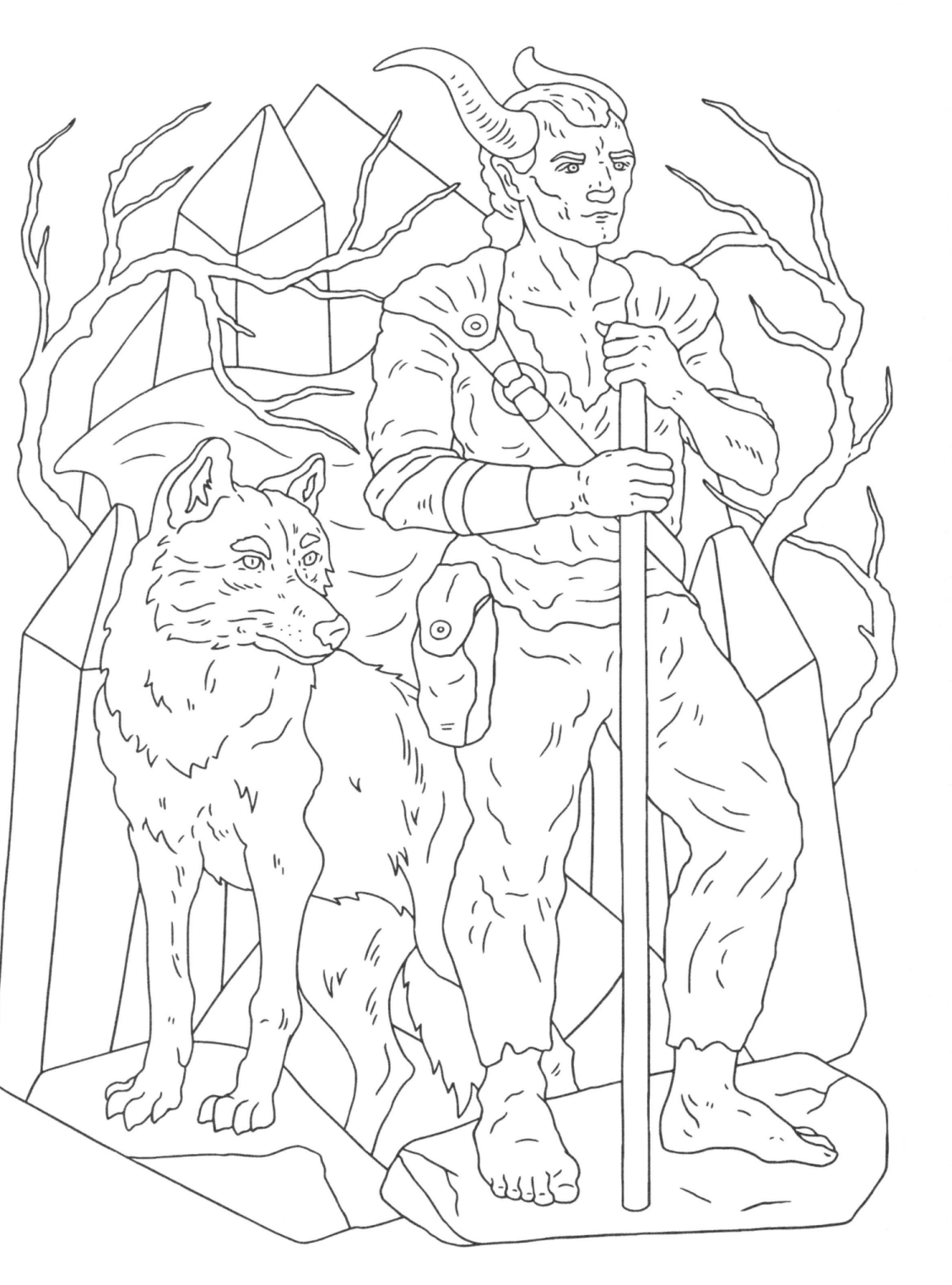

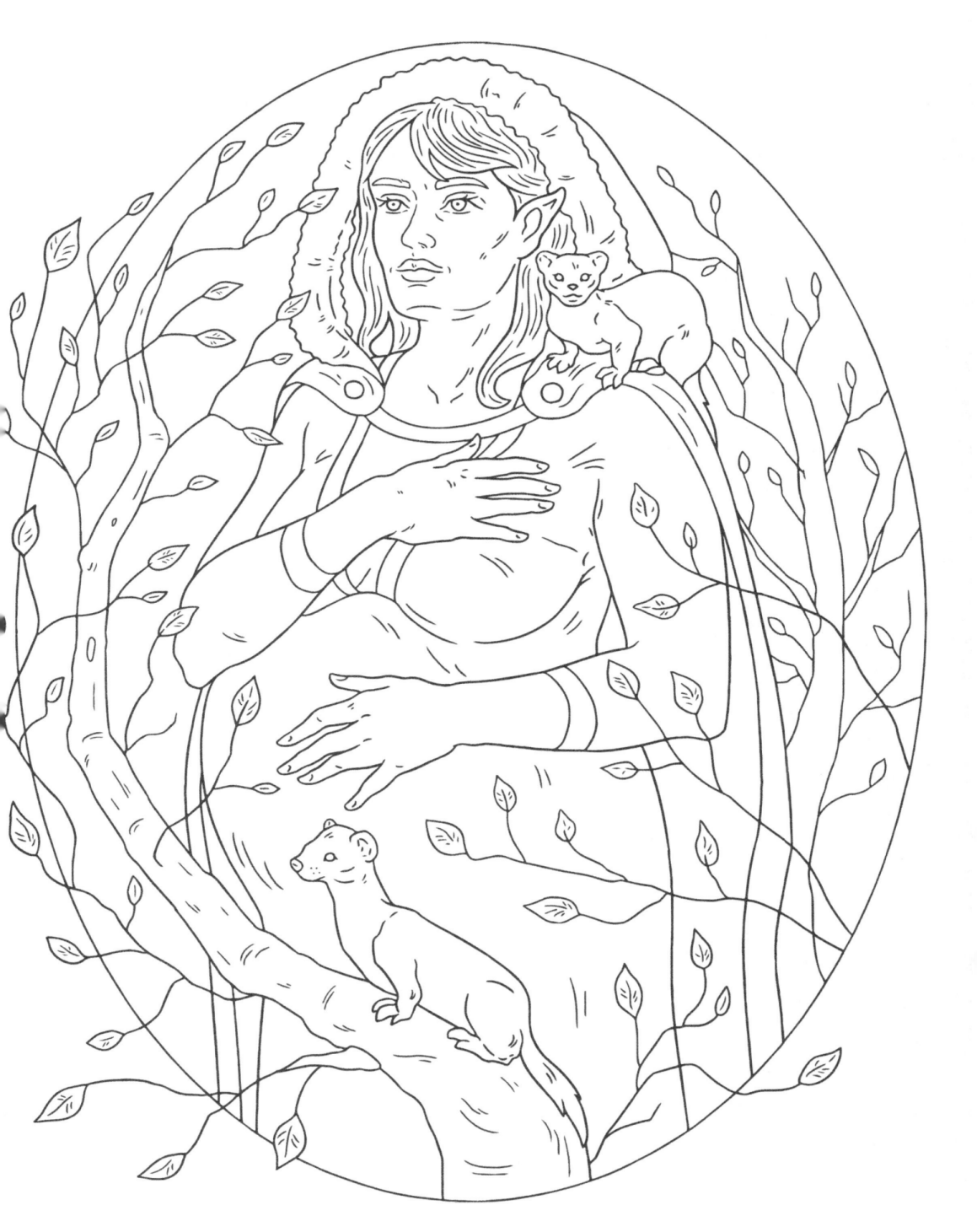

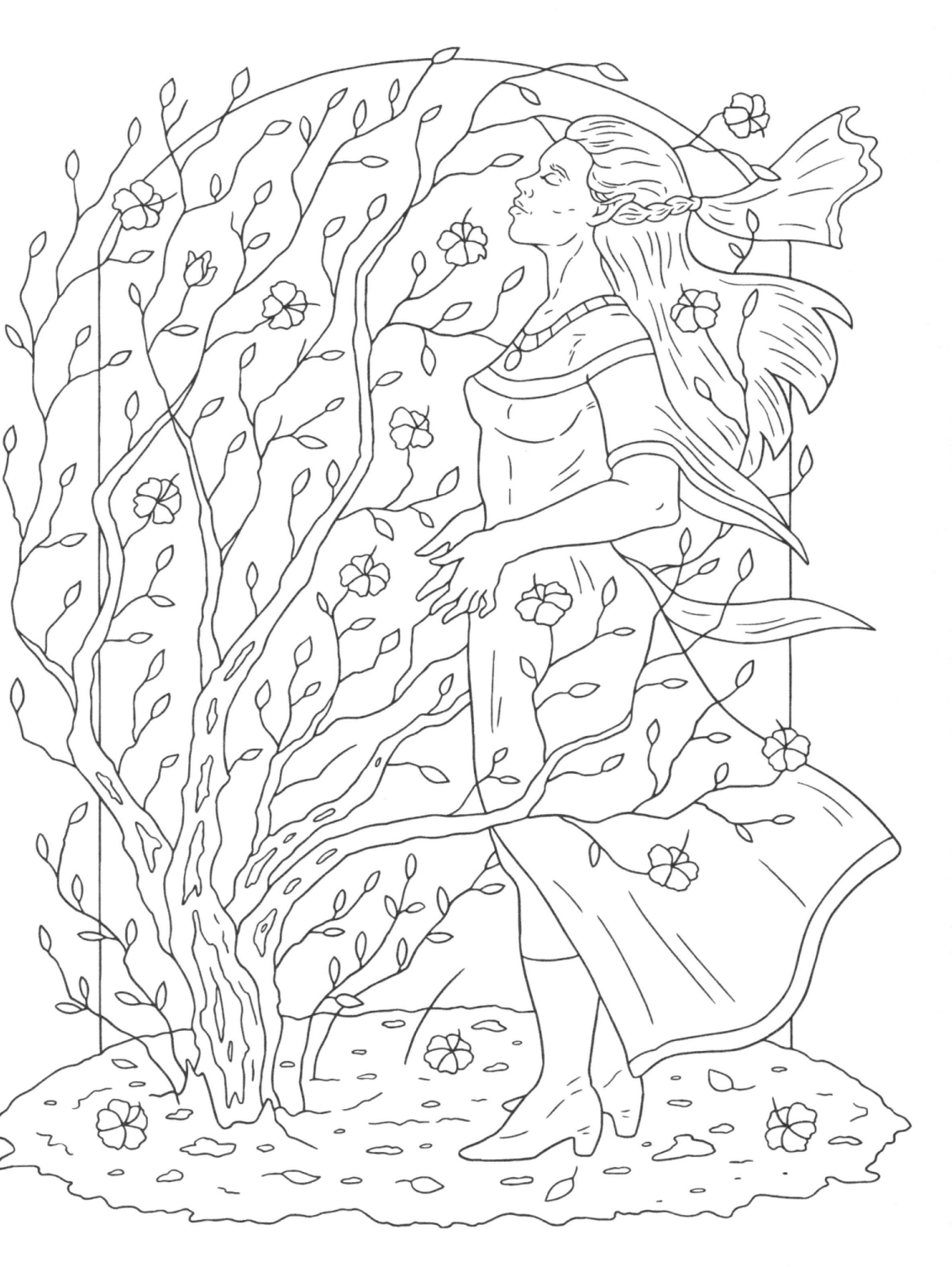

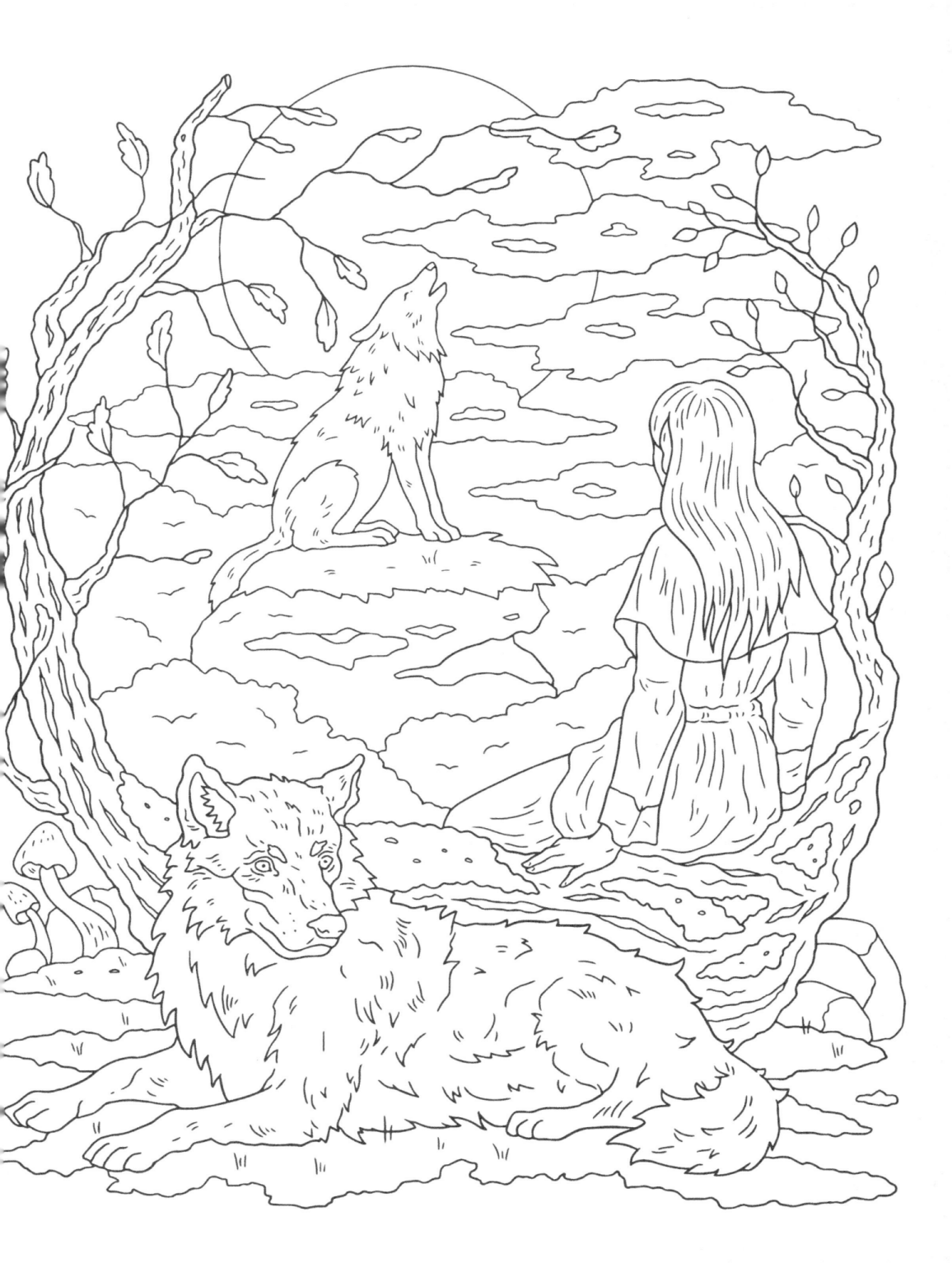

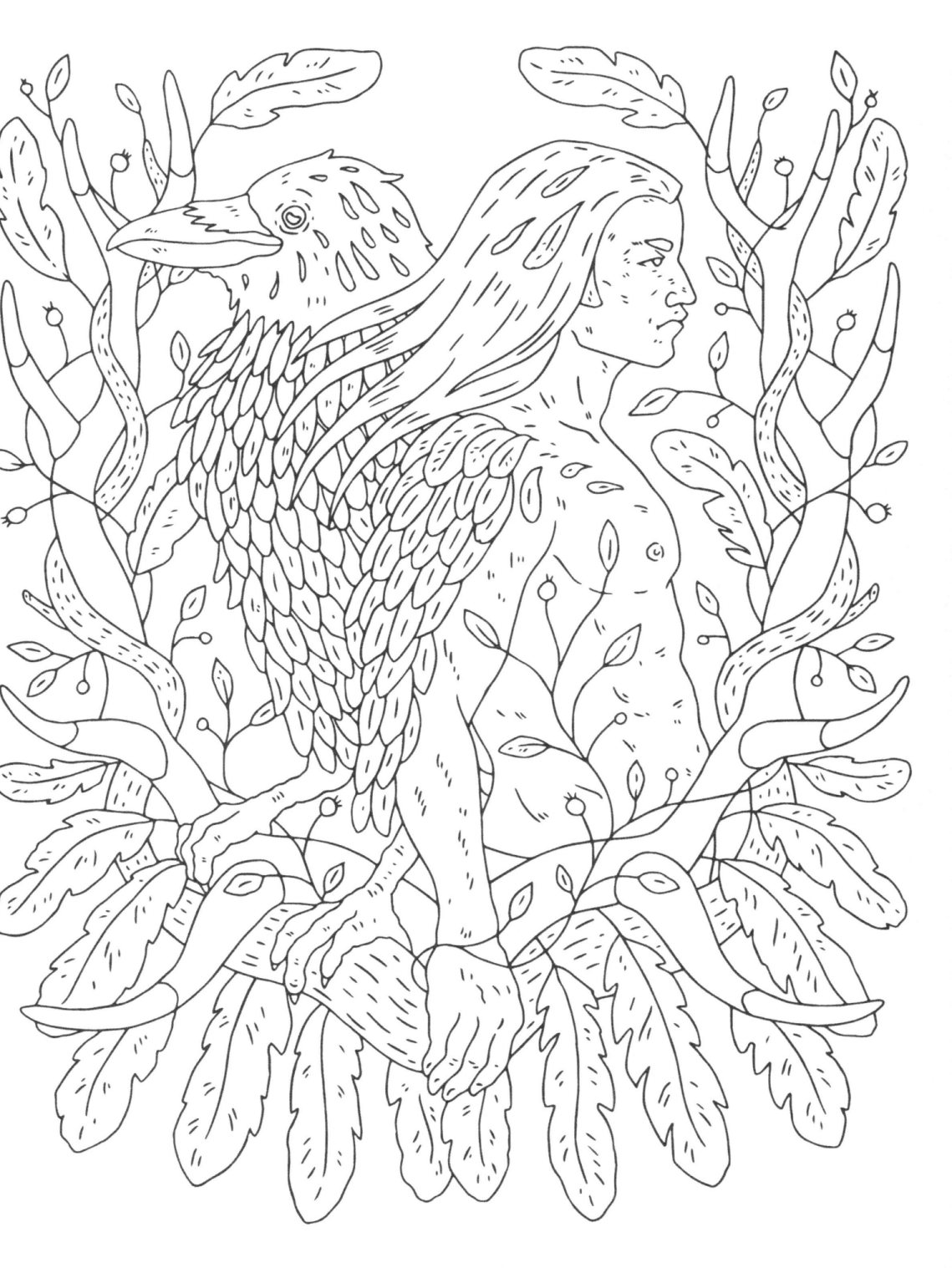

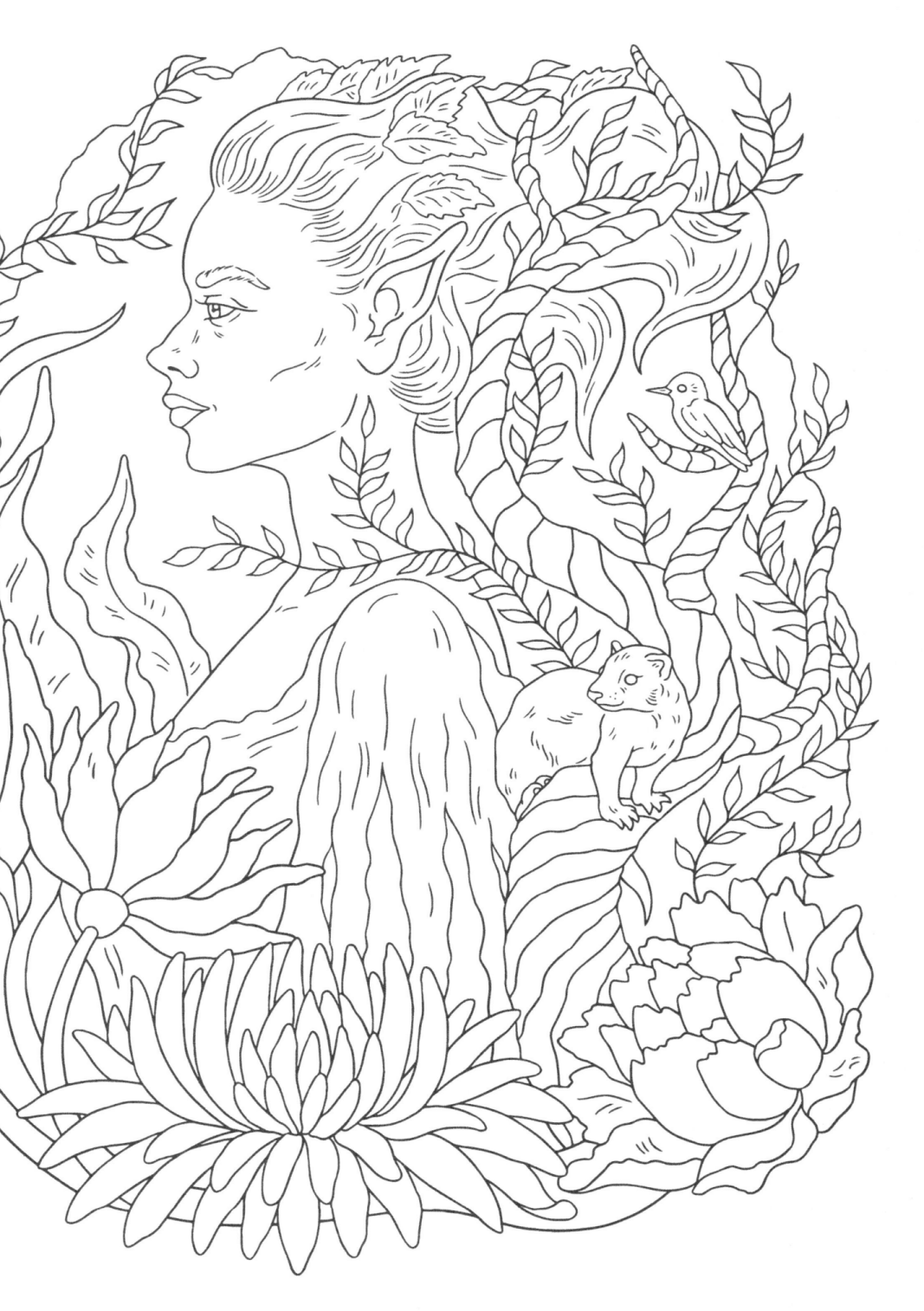

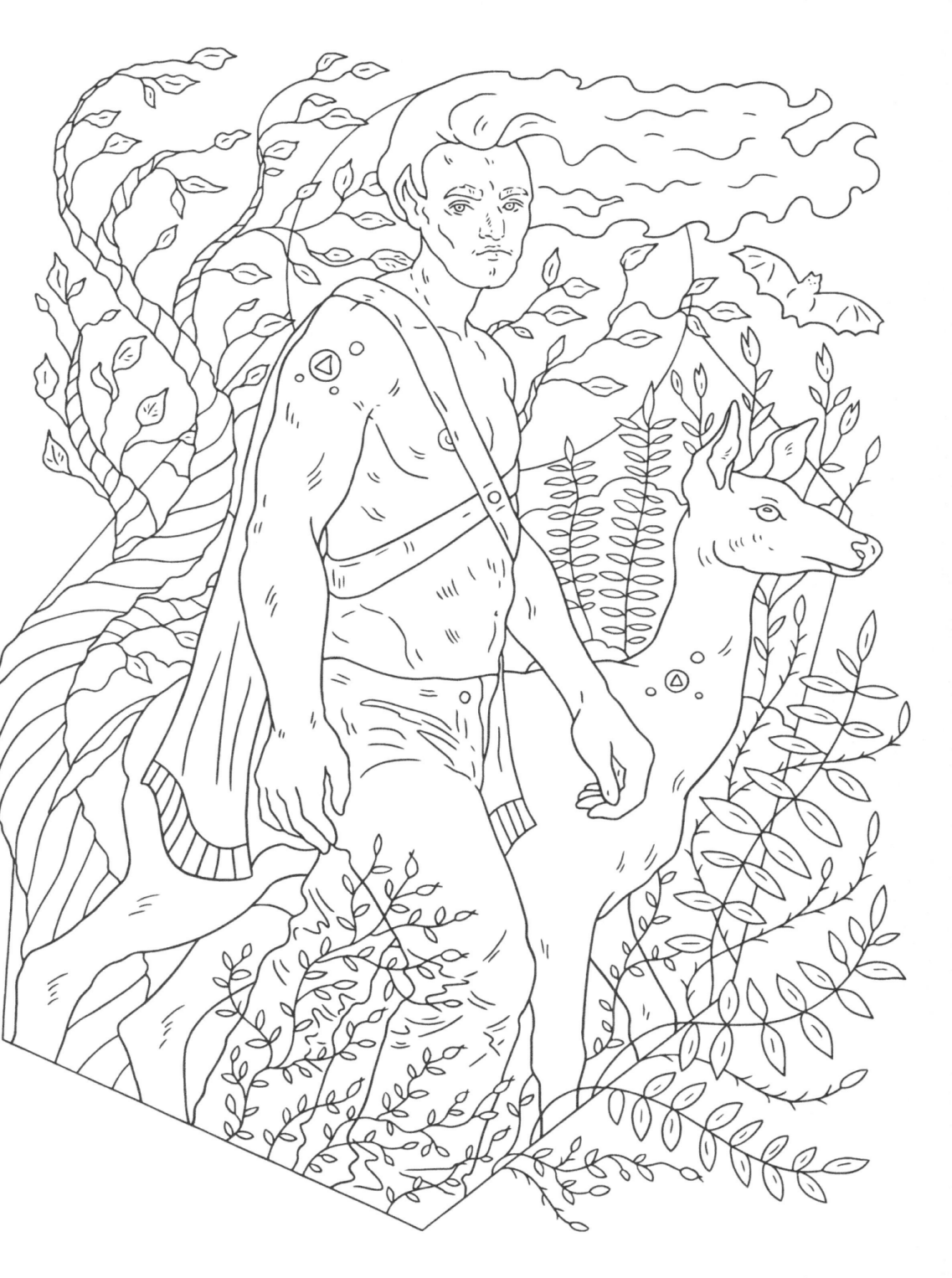

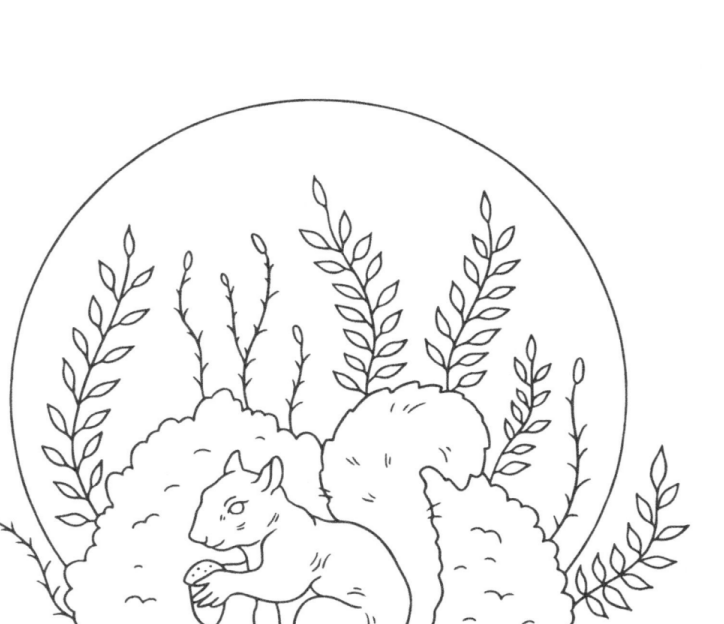

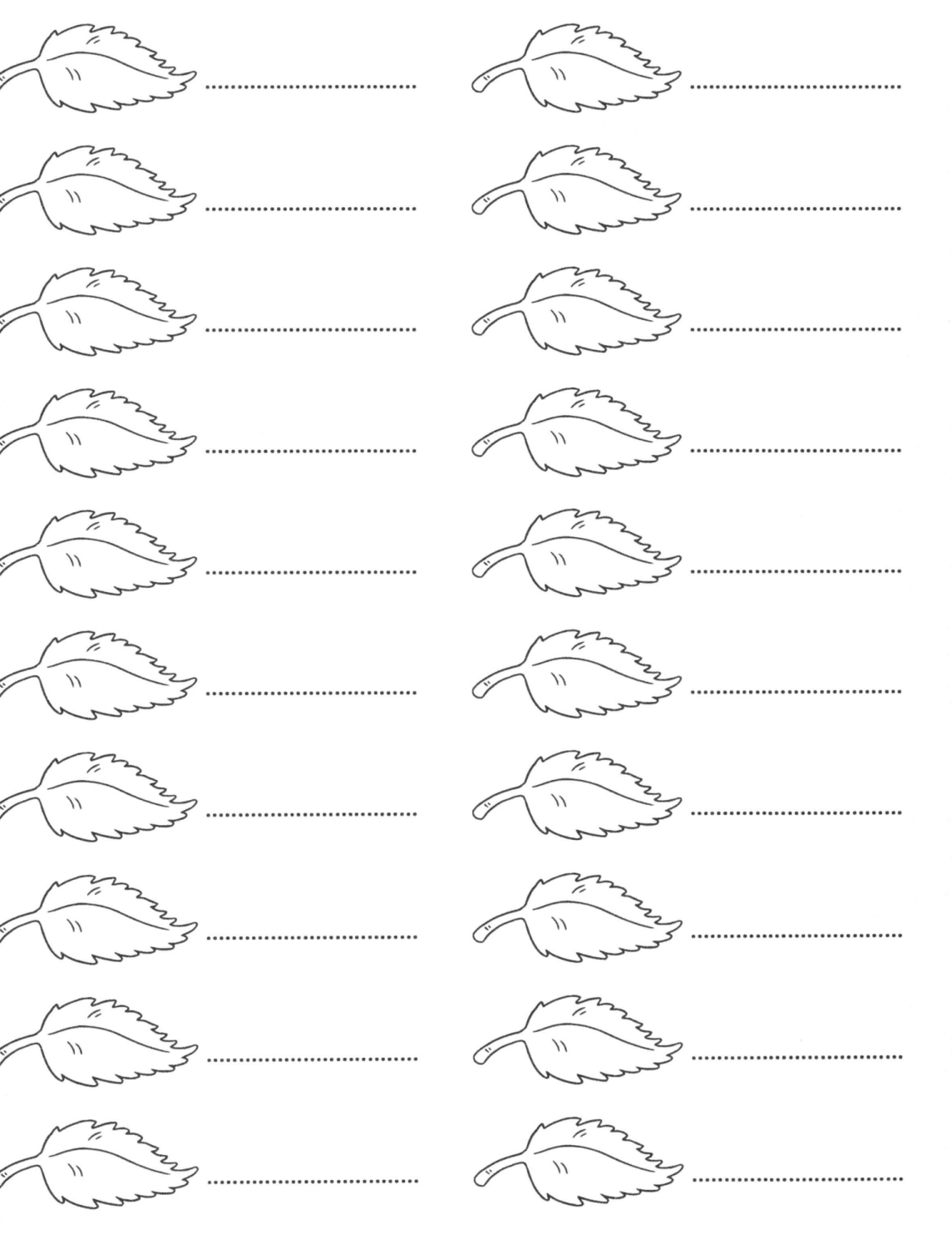

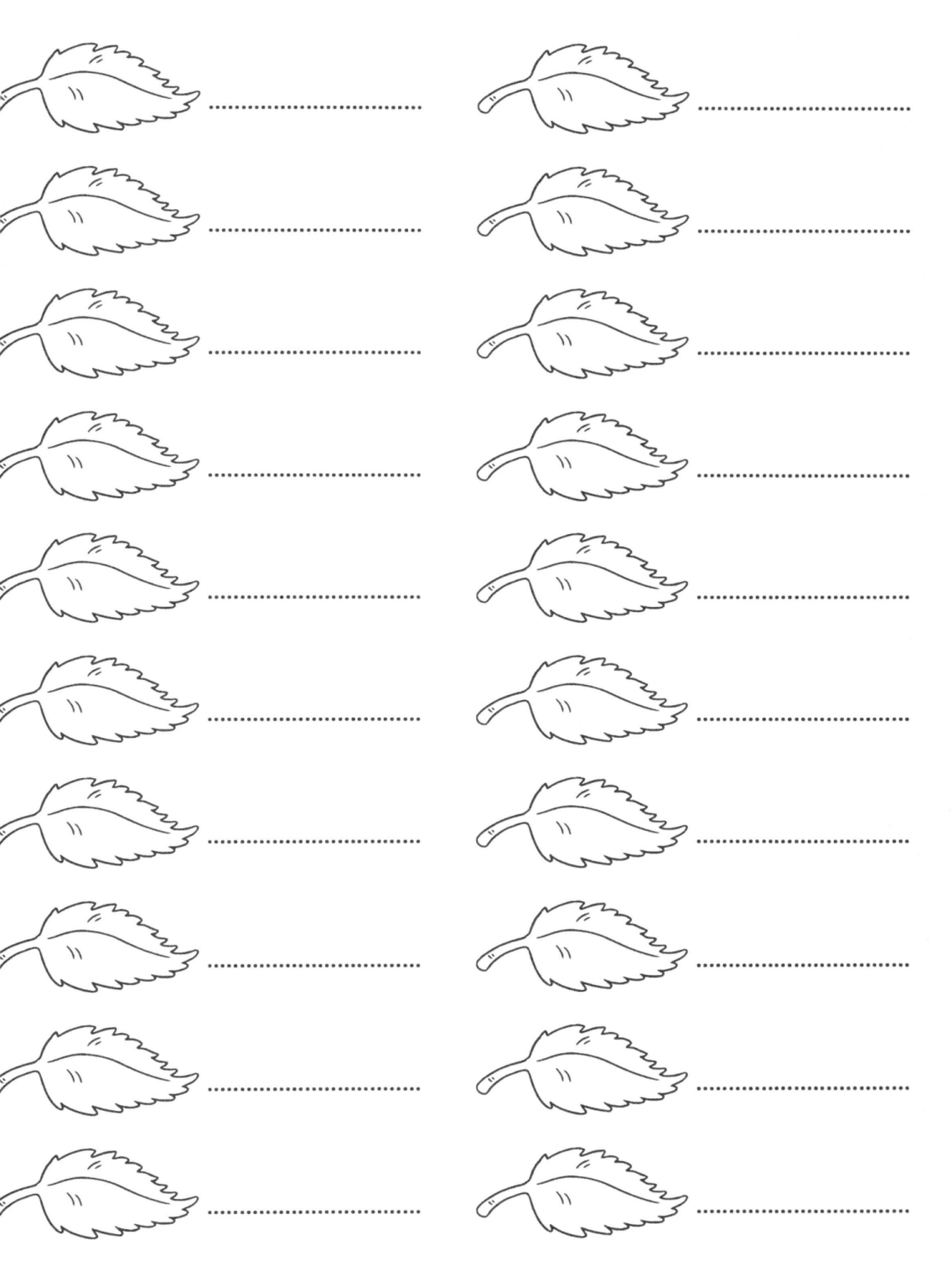

Copyright © 2019 Stremena Tuzsuzova-Petrova. All rights reserved.

No part of this content may be reproduced or transmitted without author's prior permission.

Made in the USA
Las Vegas, NV
09 December 2020

12458896R00044